Carol Marinelli recently filled in a form asking for her job title. Thrilled to be able to put down her answer, she put 'writer'. Then it asked what Carol did for relaxation, and she put down the truth—'writing'. The third question asked for her hobbies. Well, not wanting to look obsessed, she crossed her fingers and answered 'swimming'—but, given that the chlorine in the pool does terrible things to her highlights, I'm sure you can guess the real answer!

After spending three years as a die-hard New Yorker, **Kate Hewitt** now lives in a small village in the English Lake District, with her husband, their five children and a golden retriever. In addition to writing intensely emotional stories, she loves reading, baking and playing chess with her son—she has yet to win against him, but she continues to try. Learn more about Kate at kate-hewitt.com.

Discover more at millsandboon.co.uk.

THE SICILIAN'S SURPRISE LOVE-CHILD

CAROL MARINELLI

CLAIMING MY BRIDE OF CONVENIENCE

KATE HEWITT

MILLS & BOON

First Published in Great Britain 2019
by Mills & Boon, an imprint of HarperCollins*Publishers*
1 London Bridge Street, London, SE1 9GF

The Sicilian's Surprise Love-Child © 2019 by Carol Marinelli

Claiming My Bride of Convenience © 2019 by Kate Hewitt

ISBN: 978-0-263-27359-5

MIX
Paper from
responsible sources
FSC® C007454

This book is produced from independently certified FSC™ paper
to ensure responsible forest management.
For more information visit www.harpercollins.co.uk/green.

Printed and bound in Spain
by CPI, Barcelona

THE SICILIAN'S
SURPRISE
LOVE-CHILD

CAROL MARINELLI

For my great friend, Frances Housden.
Love you, Cuzzy.
C xxx

CHAPTER ONE

'AURORA WILL BE shadowing me today.'

Nico Caruso did not look up from his computer as Marianna, his PA, walked into his opulent Rome office. Instead he frowned.

'Aurora Messina from the Sicilian hotel,' Marianna elaborated, clearly assuming from Nico's frown that Aurora's was a name he did not know.

Oh, but he did.

Aurora Messina. Aged twenty-four—six years younger than him.

Aurora Eloise Messina, with her velvet brown eyes and thick dark hair that was not quite raven, though too dark to be called chestnut. Ah, yes… Aurora, with her olive skin that went pink in the sun.

'Don't you remember me, Nico?'

There was a tease in that familiar rasp to her throaty voice, and she brought with her the scent of home. The white crochet dress that she wore must have been hung out on the washing line, for it had caught not just the hot Sicilian sun but also the breeze from the ocean and the sweet scent of jasmine from her parents' garden.

'How rude of you to forget me,' Aurora continued, 'given that you have slept in my bed so many times.'

Marianna sucked in her breath at Aurora's cheeky

implication, but Nico didn't miss a beat with his dry reply, 'Ah, but never with *you* in it.'

'True…' Aurora conceded with a smile.

She had trained herself not to blush when Nico was near, but it was a struggle not to now. The stunning view of Rome panning out behind him went almost unnoticed and the lavish, expensive surroundings barely registered, for Nico, on this Monday morning, was proving more than enough for her senses to take in.

His thick black hair had been cut with skill and his strong jaw, with that slight dent in the centre, was so clean-shaven that she was actually anticipating the brief brush that would come when they shared a light cheek-to-cheek kiss.

Aurora came around the desk to greet him properly.

Of course she did.

After all, the two of them went way back.

But when Nico raised his hand to halt her approach, when his black eyes warned her not to come any closer, Aurora stepped back as if she'd been slapped.

She knew she was bolshie, and often came across as too forward, but after a lot of soul-searching as to how best to face him, she had decided to greet him as she would any old friend.

But Nico had halted her and that had hurt Aurora.

She tried not to let it show.

'Take a seat,' he told her, and then turned to his PA. 'Marianna, let's get started. We have a lot to get through.'

'First, though…' Aurora said. And instead of taking a seat, as instructed, she removed a large leather bag from her shoulder, took out a bottle of tomato sauce, and placed it on his immaculate, highly polished walnut desk. And then she took out another bottle.

'Homemade *passata* from my mother,' Aurora said, 'and here is some *limoncello* from my father.'

Nico glanced over to Marianna, who was trying to keep the shock from her expression as Aurora turned his gleaming desk into a market stall. And then his black gaze returned to Aurora.

'I don't need these,' Nico said, and gave a dismissive wave of his hand. 'You can take them back with you.'

'No!'

He had rejected her greeting. And now this!

Nico was not doing as he should. He was not saying that he missed the taste of that homemade sauce, and nor was he inviting her to join him in sharing the feast that the sauce would create.

He was not playing by the endless ingrained codes of home.

But then, she reminded herself, Nico never had.

For if that were the case then Aurora would be his wife.

Aurora Eloise Caruso.

As a teenager she had practised writing that name in her journals and saying it out loud. Now her cheeks flushed, just a little, as she tried to keep the note of anger from her voice. 'You know very well that my family would never let me visit you without gifts.'

'This is *work*—not a visit,' Nico snapped. 'You are here for five days to train for the opening of a new hotel; it is not a social occasion. Now, get these things off my desk.'

Nico knew he was being harsh, but he *had* to set the tone—and not just with Aurora.

The Silibri contingent had been in Rome for just eighteen hours and already he was fed up with the lot of them.

Francesca, who was to be Regional Manager, had brought, of all things, a salami, and left it for him at the reception desk. Did she assume that Nico could not get salami in Rome?

And Pino, who would be chief concierge at the new hotel, had somehow found his private number. Nico guessed he had got it from Aurora. He had given it to her once.

Once...

Nico refused to think of that time now.

The fact was, on their arrival yesterday evening Pino had called and asked Nico where they should go for dinner and what time he would be joining them!

Nico had rather sternly declined to do so.

The village of Silibri had come to Rome, and it seemed determined to bring him several slices of home.

Except Nico had been trying to run from home since he was sixteen.

Was it guilt or duty that always pulled him back?

He truly did not know.

'Get these off my desk, Aurora,' he repeated. It was a warning.

'But I don't want them.' She shook her head. 'I have shoes to buy, and I need the space in my suitcase.' She fixed him with narrowed eyes. 'Assuming I'm allowed to shop during non-work hours?'

He almost smiled at her sarcastic tone, but did not.

A smile.

A kiss.

When combined with Aurora, Nico knew full well the trouble they made...

So he met her glare with one of his own and hoped she'd hear the message in his veiled words. 'When you're not working, Aurora, I don't care what you do.'

'Good.'

'For now...' Nico flicked his hand at the desk. '... can we get rid of these and start work? We're already running behind.'

'I'll take them.'

Marianna was rarely flustered as she was now. Aurora had that effect on people.

'And I'll get the swatches for the meeting...'

'Swatches?' Nico checked.

'It's decision day for the Silibri uniforms.'

'What decision?' Nico inhaled deeply and tried not to show his irritation. *Really?* Since when did he get involved in orders for uniforms?

'They don't like the green,' Marianna said.

'But it's the same as in all my hotels. I want continuity—'

Nico halted himself, deciding that he would save it for the meeting. He nodded to Marianna, who gathered the bottles and, with Nico's desk back to its usual order, headed out.

He was surprised when Aurora did not follow, and instead took a seat. 'I thought you were supposed to be shadowing Marianna?'

Aurora could hear the irritation beneath the silk of his low tone and she spoke hurriedly. 'I wanted a moment alone to apologise for being indiscreet. I was making a little joke about the times when you used to stay at our house.'

She grimaced then, because despite her best efforts that hadn't come out right. There really wasn't anything to make a joke about. Her father had used to find the young Nico asleep in the park after a beating from his father and had insisted he come and sleep at their home. Aurora would be moved to a made-up bed at the foot of her parents' and Nico would be given her room.

'Apology accepted,' Nico said, and got back to his spreadsheets.

He was still angry, though, Aurora knew, and she was cross with herself too, for she had been so determined to be serene when she saw him.

Nico did not make her feel serene.

'Anyway…' Aurora continued, and under the desk she gave his knee a playful little tap with her foot. 'We were never in bed together—you took my virginity on the couch!'

Her breath hitched as he caught her ankle with his hand and gripped it tight for a second. She wished—how she wished—that he would run that hand up her calf, but he scolded her instead.

'I didn't *take* it, Aurora. You very willingly gave it to me.' He pointedly removed her foot and released his grip. 'You *pleaded* with me, in fact.' He turned back to the computer. 'It's forgotten now.'

Liar.

For Nico, sex was necessary and frequent—if a touch emotionless. And it was always a smooth and controlled affair, taking place in his suite at the hotel, never at his home.

It did not compare to the panting, hot, sweaty coupling that had taken place with Aurora.

Nothing could ever compare.

'Forgotten?' Aurora checked.

'It happened just the once and it was a long time ago.'

'Four years, Nico.'

Yes, it had been four years since that night, and Nico had been paying for it ever since.

That one slip had cost him millions.

Tens of millions, in fact.

Though the cost of a new hotel had been preferable to another night under the Messina roof.

He did not glance up as she stood and walked to the window.

This was hell.

Nico was aware he had treated her terribly.

He should never have slept with her.

They had been supposed to marry. Of course they had never had a say in it, but as they'd grown up it had become a given. Her *nonna*'s house had been left to her father, Bruno, and he had kept it for them to reside in after their wedding day.

Nico had been able to think of nothing worse. Stuck in that damned village, living opposite the in-laws and working all day on the vines.

Aurora had taken it well when he'd told her they would never marry. She had laughed and said something along the lines of *Thank God for that*.

It had been the sun that had made her eyes sparkle, Nico told himself. She had been sixteen then, and a skinny, slip of a girl. He hadn't seen her for a few years after that.

Oh, but when he had…

He glanced over to where she stood, looking out towards the Vatican City, and though he wanted to turn back to his computer screen he could not resist a double-take.

There was nothing, Nico thought, more beautiful than a beautiful Sicilian woman.

She was dark-eyed and dark-haired, with voluptuous curves that had never seen a gym let alone a scalpel or silicone. Beneath her full bust in the white crochet dress there was a thin strap of leather, tied in a bow.

He could think of no other woman who might look so sexy in such a dress, but she certainly did. He wanted to pull on that bow...he wanted to bare her breasts and pull her onto his knee. To kiss that mouth and properly welcome her to Rome.

His eyes drifted down to her shoes, which were neutral. Her legs, though, were not—their olive skin was bare and her calves were toned. His gaze followed the line of her long limbs until it rested where he knew he would find dark silken curls; he knew, too, the grip of those thighs.

She was fire. And he must do all he could not to let it catch him. For what Nico craved in his life was order.

Aurora could feel his eyes on her and she liked the vague, unsettled feeling that tightened low in her stomach and brought a hot and heavy sensation between her legs.

She had seen him since that fateful night—of course she had. But since the morning after they had never been alone.

Now, for a few precious moments, they were.

Aurora had practised this moment in her head and in the mirror so many times, and had sworn to rein herself in. But what had she gone and done?

Teased and cajoled and tried to draw a reaction from this cold immutable man, who had ruined her for anyone else.

Yet she could not bring herself to regret losing her virginity to him. Aurora would never regret that.

She attempted a more bland conversation. 'I like Rome...'

'Good.'

'Though I *love* it in the early morning. I went exploring this morning...'

Nico looked back to his computer screen.

'I felt as if I had the city all to myself. Well, not quite...'

She thought of the cafés and markets opening, and the street cleaners she had encountered on her early-morning walk—the walk during which she had promised herself that when she saw Nico later she would be serene and controlled. Sophisticated. Like the slender beauties he dated, whom she read about while bile churned in her stomach.

'Tonight we're all going on a bus tour...' She halted, thinking how touristy and gauche she must sound to him. 'Are you excited about the Silibri opening?' she asked, because that seemed safe.

'I will be glad when it's done.'

Glad when he would be able to hand it over to his executive and the managers. When it would be up and running and no longer at this intense stage.

Right now, though, the tension was all in his office.

It was a relief when Marianna appeared and, with Aurora observing, they began to go through his schedule.

Nico was to meet with the Silibri hotel staff in fifteen minutes, and after that his day was back-to-back meetings with accountants, financiers and lawyers—and, no, Nico said, he would not be staying at the hotel that night.

'You have a breakfast meeting at seven and the helicopter is booked for nine...' Marianna frowned at this slight anomaly. 'Usually you stay here if you're flying out.'

'I'll be residing at home tonight,' Nico said. 'Now, can we check my Silibri schedule? I want to see my father's doctor as soon as I arrive.'

'You're going home…?' Aurora blinked. 'Why are you going home when we are all *here*?'

'Again…' Nico sighed. 'You are here for staff training.'

He looked to Marianna and was grateful when she stepped in.

'Signor Caruso and I run through his schedule each morning, Aurora. This is not a meeting, and nor is it a discussion; it is to ensure that everything is in order and that we are both clear on timings.'

'Of course…' Aurora attempted, but there were a million questions in her eyes about why he was leaving Rome so soon after they had arrived.

Nico answered none of them.

Instead, having gone through his impossibly busy week, they headed out of his office, with Nico holding the door for both the women.

'After you,' Nico said.

He wished his good manners were not quite so ingrained, and that he did not have to hold open the door, for the scent of her reached him again. The chemistry that flared between them was undeniable, and the want was still there.

Nico, though, was first to walk into the boardroom.

The Silibri contingent were there, waiting, and they greeted him warmly.

Too warmly.

'Hey, Nico!'

And there were *more* gifts set out on the table.

Amongst other things, Francesca had brought homemade *biscotti* to go with the coffee being served. Only Vincenzo, his marketing manager, sat rigid, clearly taken back by the party-like atmosphere in the room.

He smoothed his auburn hair nervously and cast a

slightly aghast look at Nico. Bizarrely, for the briefest of seconds, Nico wanted to tell Vincenzo to relax. Did he not know how things worked in Sicily? Did he not know that humour and conversation were an art form there, especially in Silibri?

Of course not. Vincenzo had been brought in from the Florence branch.

'Let's get started,' Nico said.

It would hopefully be a quick meeting.

Aurora was to be assistant manager of marketing. It was not something she had studied for, but she knew the area well and loved taking photos—and she had ideas. Many of them.

Nico hadn't actually got her the job; she did not need him to succeed.

Well, maybe a bit...

For without him there would be no hotel.

Vincenzo was speaking of the excitement locally, and said there were a few interviews nationally, for various tourism shows and breakfast television and the like.

'I shall handle those,' Vincenzo said.

'You can take turns with Aurora,' Nico interjected.

'But I have had media training,' Vincenzo pointed out. 'Aurora can be a touch...forceful, and we want to extend a gentle invitation.'

'Vincenzo,' Nico said. 'I wasn't offering a suggestion, I was *telling* you to take turns with Aurora.'

He was not doing her any favours. Vincenzo was vain and self-serving—and, though he was brilliant at his job, it was as clear as day to Nico that Aurora, with her passion, her low throaty laugh, with her sheer love of Silibri, would be more enticing for potential guests.

'Next,' Nico said, and nodded to Francesca.

'The fittings for the uniforms have been delayed.'

'Then get them done,' Nico said, even while knowing it wasn't going to be as easy as that.

'I have tried, but the staff have issues with the colour.'

'And the fabric...' It was the first time Aurora had spoken. 'The wool is too heavy and the green makes us look like...' She snapped her fingers. 'That Englishman's Merry Men.'

Nico had to think for a moment. But then he always had to think when Aurora was around—she brought him no peace.

He thought of the dark green uniforms that looked so elegant against the old Roman and sophisticated Florentine buildings, and worked well in both England and France, and then he joined the dots she had led him to with her mention of 'the Englishman's Merry Men'.

'You mean Robin Hood?'

'Who?' Aurora frowned, and then she gave him a tiny smile to say of *course* she knew who he meant and was teasing him.

Their minds jostled, and she could see he was fighting not to return her smile. She was still looking at Nico's full mouth, with a smile on her own, when Vincenzo cleared his throat and spoke up.

'We think that Silibri should have a more casual feel.'

'It's a five-star hotel.' Nico gave a shake of his head. 'I do *not* want my staff looking casual.'

'Of course not,' Vincenzo agreed. 'But there is a stunning French navy linen, and teamed with crisp white shirts...'

'We would look like sailors,' Aurora sulked.

Nico pressed the bridge of his nose between finger and thumb. What the hell had he been thinking? What had possessed him to venture into Silibri? He should have sold the land there and been done with it…

Yet as he sat there he recalled Aurora's emphatic *no* when he had suggested that the night after—

Damn, no matter how he tried to avoid it, all roads led to that night.

Nico forced himself back to the moment: What in God's name was he doing, sitting here discussing fabric? It was *his* hotel and it had been four years in the making.

The trouble with the Silibri venture was that the staff considered it to be *their* hotel too. They were all *so* involved and took it all *so* personally.

'What about the same green as the other hotels, but in linen?' Francesca suggested.

Aurora shook her head.

'That just takes us back to the Merry Men,'

'So what do *you* suggest, Aurora?' Nico threw down his pen in exasperation.

Of course she had an immediate answer. 'Persian Orange.'

From her seemingly bottomless bag she produced several swatches of fabric and proceeded to pass them around. It was a linen blend that wouldn't crease, she assured them, and with one look Nico knew she was right.

'It is the colour of the temple ruins and the monastery just before sunset,' Aurora said. 'And you know how beautiful Silibri looks at that time of night. Mother Nature chose her colours wisely.'

'It is a bold colour,' Vincenzo objected. 'A touch too bold, perhaps?'

'I don't agree that it is too bold; it is, in fact, quite plain,' Aurora refuted, then cocked her head to the side.

Nico watched as her knowing eyes weighed up Vincenzo.

'Are you worried that it might clash with your red hair?'

'Of course not...' Vincenzo was flustered and smoothed said red hair down.

'Because,' Aurora continued, 'we could have bespoke shades on the same theme, with Persian Orange being the main one.'

'*Bespoke* shades...?' Vincenzo checked.

And Nico watched silently as his marketing manager warmed to his new assistant's idea, and watched, too, Aurora's small, self-satisfied smile as of course she got her way.

Heaven help Vincenzo, Nico thought, trying to manage her. Because Aurora could not be managed nor contained.

She was as Sicilian as Mount Etna, as volatile as the volcano it was famous for, and she could not be beguiled or easily charmed. She was perceptive and assiduous and...

And he refused to give in to her ways.

'I'll consider it,' Nico said.

'Consider it?' Aurora checked. 'But what is there to consider when it's perfect?'

'There is plenty to consider,' Nico snapped. 'Next.'

It had been scheduled as a thirty-minute meeting but in the end it took sixty-three—and of course it did not end there.

As Marianna disappeared for a quick restroom break, and Nico attempted to stalk off, Aurora caught up with him. 'I wonder if we could speak? I have an idea.'

'It has all been said in the meeting.'

'This isn't about the uniforms. I have another idea for the Silibri hotel.'

'Then speak with Vincenzo, your manager.'

'Why would I share my idea with *him*?'

'Because I don't generally deal with assistants.'

Aurora felt his cool, snobbish dismissal and told him so. 'It is spring, Nico, and the sun is shining—yet you are so cold that when I stand near you I shiver.'

'Then get a coat! Aurora, let me make something very clear—and this is a conversation that you can repeat to all your colleagues. You are here for a week of training to find out how *I* like things done and how *I* want my hotel to operate. You're *not* here for little chats and suggestions, and catch-ups and drinks. I did *not* build a hotel in Silibri to expand my social life.'

Nico wanted this conversation to be over.

'You are shadowing Marianna for the rest of the day?' he checked.

'*Si?*'

'Then what are you doing standing in mine?'

CHAPTER TWO

DAMN YOU, NICO!

How much clearer could he have made it that he did not want her near him? He could not have been more horrible had he tried.

As Nico stalked off Aurora wanted to be done with her feelings for him. To shed them. To discard them. To stamp her foot on them and kick them to the kerb. She was tired of them and bone-weary from this unrequited love.

'Aurora.' Marianna had found her. 'We need to talk. Or rather, you need to listen.'

'I already know what you're going to say.'

But she was told anyway.

A little more decorum and a lot less sass, or she would be shadowing the bottle-washer for the rest of the week.

And while Aurora understood what was being said, she just did not know how to squeeze herself into the box demanded of her. Or how *not* to be herself when she was near Nico.

'Hello, husband,' she had used to greet him teasingly when, as a young girl, she had opened the door to him.

He would shake his head and roll his eyes at the precocious child who constantly fought for his smile and attention. 'Your father says he wants some firewood chopped,' Nico would respond.

Yet, as much as he'd dismiss her, she would still sit and watch him chop firewood, and her heart would bleed when he took off his top and she saw a new bruise or a gash on his back.

How could Geo do that to him?

How could anyone hate Nico so?

Then he would look over, and sometimes he would smile rather than scowl at his devoted audience. And her day would be made.

Nico hadn't broken her heart when he had first left Silibri—after all, she had only been ten then—though for a while she had cried herself to sleep at night.

No, the heartbreak had occurred on one of his rare trips home, when Aurora had been sixteen.

Her heart had sung, just at knowing he was home, and then one afternoon he had spoken at length with her father behind closed doors. She had assumed they were drinking the grappa her father had saved for this very day.

And then Nico had come out and asked if she'd like to take a walk. She had quickly washed her face and hands and scrubbed her nails, so her hands would look pretty for the ring. And she had brushed her teeth for she had wanted to taste fresh for her first kiss.

They had walked down the hill and around the old monastery, but instead of heading to the ancient temple ruins, Aurora's favourite place, Nico had suggested they take the steps down the cliff to the beach.

'Our fathers are very old fashioned…' Nico had said as they walked on the deserted sands.

'Yes!' Aurora had beamed, for she had known he had just been speaking with hers.

'They try to make decisions for us.'

She'd felt the first prickle of warning that this conversation might not be going as she had long hoped. 'They do,' she had rather carefully agreed.

'Aurora, I stopped allowing my father to dictate to me a long time ago.'

'I know he is difficult. I know you hate him. But—'

'Aurora,' he broke in. 'I can't see myself ever marrying. I don't want to have a family. I want freedom...'

It had been the worst moment of her life.

'Aurora!'

Marianna's voice broke in on her painful reminiscence.

'Are you even listening to what I'm saying?'

'Of course,' Aurora said. She hadn't been listening, but she could guess very well what Marianna had said. 'Don't worry, I...' She gave a slow nod, took a deep breath and made a vow—not just to Marianna but also to herself. 'I will not embarrass myself again.'

Aurora was done with Nico Caruso.

For eight years she had loved him in secret.

A whole third of her life!

Well, no more.

It was time to snuff out the torch she carried.

She would be calm and distant and professional if she ever saw him again.

'I didn't mean you to take it like that...' Marianna gave her first kind smile. 'Nico is a wonderful boss, but he's no one's friend. Just remember that when you're working together.'

'I will.'

'Come on—the driver is waiting.'

'The driver?'

'So I can go and pack for Signor Caruso's trip. Oh,

and I must organise his driver for the morning, now he's no longer staying at the hotel...'

Aurora just wanted the day to be over. She wanted to go back to her hotel room, throw herself on the bed and cry...and then emerge better and stronger and step into the future without him.

Instead, she had to step into his home.

It was beautiful, of course.

Nico lived in the Parioli district, and his residence was just a short drive from the hotel. It was elegant and tasteful and her heels rang out on the marble floors.

There was a huge gleaming kitchen, where Marianna deposited the *limoncello* and *passata* in rather empty cupboards. Then they went back to the main corridor, with its cathedral-high ceilings and a grand staircase which she climbed reluctantly—for surely Nico's bedroom was not the best place to attempt to get over him?

The master bedroom had French windows and a balcony and looked out to Villa Borghese Park. And, had it not been Nico's bedroom that she stood in, Aurora might have been tempted to step out onto the balcony and drink in the view. Instead she looked at the vast bed, dressed in white with dark cushions, and imagined Nico beneath the crisp linen.

His bedroom daunted and overwhelmed her, although Marianna was clearly very used to it and quickly pulled out a suit carrier and a case and started to select shirts and suits.

'Aurora, could you please sort out underwear?'

Joy!

It was agony—sheer agony— Once, a long time ago, she had slipped her hand inside similar black silk boxers and felt his velvet skin...

Oh, it killed her to be in his bedroom, and to remember how it had been between them, but she tried hard to keep her vow and focus on work.

'Should I pack these?' Aurora asked, holding up a pair of black lounge pants. To her surprise, Marianna laughed.

'No, I bought those just in case he has to go into hospital or something.'

'Oh…'

'You have to think of all eventualities if you're a PA.'

Except Aurora didn't want to be one. 'Marianna, why am I shadowing you today? I'm enjoying it, of course, but I thought I would stay with the marketing team.'

Marianna put the suit she was holding down on the bed before answering. 'Well, I don't always travel with Signor Caruso and, given that he'll presumably be spending some considerable time in Silibri, I thought it might be prudent to train someone to assist me when he's there. I have someone in each of his hotels with whom I liaise. I spoke with Francesca and she suggested you.'

'*I* would be Nico's PA?'

'No. But I want someone in the Silibri hotel that I can liaise with directly regarding him.'

'Does Nico know about this?'

'No, it's just something Francesca and I have discussed. I would not trouble Signor Caruso unless I considered it viable…' She gave a thin smile, which told Aurora that she was already having her doubts as to her suitability for the role.

Aurora had doubts of her own.

Getting closer to Nico wasn't going to snuff out the torch. Instead it would fan the eternal flame that burned for him. So Aurora said the bravest thing she could. 'It

is very nice of you to consider me—but, no.' Aurora
shook her head. 'I don't think that role would be for me.'

Tonight, when she was back in the hotel, she would
cry one final time over him, Aurora decided.

There would be no bus tour.

She was a little tired of being with her friends. They
saw each other every day and they were all so much
older than she.

No, tonight she would recall with shame her own
behaviour earlier with Nico and then she would weep
into the pillow. And then...

Well, it was time she moved on—time she started
dating.

Time to flirt.

To be twenty-four and single in Rome.

She might even download the dating app that Chi-
Chi and Antonietta had told her about!

*To hell with you, Nico Caruso, because I want to
be with a man who wants me. I am finally out of your
shadow.*

And she was soon to be out of Marianna's.

'Where's Aurora?' Nico asked late in the day.

'Oh, she's with the marketing team,' Marianna said
and then glanced at the time. 'Though they'll all be off
on their bus tour now.'

Nico gave a small eye-roll, though not with any mal-
ice. It was more in amusement that Pino had called and
invited him to join them.

Again he had declined.

'Do you know?' Marianna said. 'I have never met
a more enthusiastic lot of people. With their energy
and exuberance I'm sure the new hotel is going to be
amazing.'

'If you like Persian Orange,' Nico said, and he pushed over the uniform order he had signed off on. Persian Orange! With bespoke tones of Butterscotch and Burnt Caramel for those who felt the shade might not suit their colouring.

Nico had a headache from looking at so much orange.

And he had another question. 'Why was Aurora shadowing you today? I thought her role was in marketing.'

'Correct,' Marianna agreed. 'But presumably you will be spending a lot of time in Silibri…?'

'Not once the hotel is up and running.'

'You are always between hotels. I have Teresa in Florence, Amelie in France… Francesca thought that Aurora might be suitable—'

'No.' Nico said it too fast, and with too much force, and he attempted a quick recovery. 'Look, I'm sure Aurora will be excellent in her marketing role, but I don't think she would work out as—'

'It's fine,' Marianna cut in. 'Aurora said the same.'

'She did?'

Why did that feel like a punch to his guts rather than spread relief? And why did the thought of working closely with Aurora unsettle him so?

Nico grabbed his jacket and took the elevator down to head for home.

He did not need to ponder further to know the answer: there was *way* too much history between them.

CHAPTER THREE

The night that neither can forget...

'YOU CAN TELL Nico that I'm not leaving my home.'

Just hearing Nico's father say his name had Aurora's heart both soaring and shattering anew.

It was a regular occurrence in Silibri. Nico Caruso's name was mentioned often.

'Since when did I have a direct line to your son, Geo?' Determined not to give herself away, Aurora responded light-heartedly as she plumped the old man's cushions behind him. 'I haven't spoken to Nico in ages.'

'He's sending his helicopter to take me to Rome.'

Aurora's cushion plumping was paused for a moment.

Geo got confused at times, and was also known to exaggerate, but even by Geo's standards this was too far-fetched to be believed.

'Who told you that?' Aurora asked as he rested back in his chair and she straightened up.

'The doctor did.'

'Oh? And is this the same doctor who told you that your drinking would kill you?' Aurora checked.

Geo gave a reluctant smile.

'The same doctor who said that you couldn't manage here alone and needed to be in a nursing home?' she continued. 'Because I thought you told me that that doctor could not be believed.'

'Perhaps,' Geo conceded, 'but he was telling the truth this time—Nico is sending a helicopter to fetch me.'

Wildfires had been ravaging the south coast of Sicily and steadily working their way towards their small village for more than a week. They had been told to get out—of course they had—but, like Geo, her father had refused.

She didn't doubt that Nico wanted his father away from the fires, but a private helicopter was *way* beyond a boy from Silibri—even a successful one!

Geo's lies were becoming more and more extreme. A few weeks ago, when Aurora had dropped off his shopping, he had told her that she had just missed seeing Maria. Maria, Geo's wife and Nico's mother, had died the year Aurora had been born—some twenty years ago.

Last week he had said that Nico owned three hotels across Europe. When Aurora had refused to believe him, Geo had corrected himself: Nico owned *four*!

'He stole from me!' Geo said now, and cursed. 'He took what was mine.'

'You tell tall tales, Geo,' Aurora said gently.

'Well, he can stick his nursing home in Rome. I hate him. Why would I want to live closer to him?'

Aurora knew that father and son did not get on. She knew it very well.

But, though she loathed Geo's treatment of Nico, she could not walk past the old man's house and not drop in. It was worth it if it made things a little easier on Nico to know that his father was being cared for.

'Now,' Aurora said. 'Is there anything else that you need me to do?'

'Take some money from my dresser and run down to the store.'

'I'm not getting you whisky, Geo,' Aurora told him.

'Why not? We're all going to die in these fires!'

Aurora beamed. 'Then you will meet your maker sober.'

'Take the money and get me my whisky.'

'Don't.'

The very deep voice caused Aurora's stomach to flip over, but even before she turned to face its direction she knew its source.

'Nico...' she said. 'You're here?'

'Yes.'

He wore suit trousers and a white shirt—which somehow, despite the ash floating in the air, looked fresh. His hair was black and clean, unlike hers, which felt heavy after a day spent sweeping leaves outside Geo's home and trying to get his house as safe as possible.

Oh, *why* couldn't he have arrived in a couple of hours, when she was all washed and dressed up for Antonietta's party?

But, really, what did it matter? Nico would never look at her in *that* way.

'How did you get here?' Aurora asked. 'The road from the airport is closed.'

'I came by helicopter,' Nico said.

'Told you,' Geo declared to Aurora, but then he addressed his son. 'I'm not going anywhere and you're not welcome here. Get out!'

Here we go, Aurora thought, and sure enough, within two minutes of Nico arriving, Geo was shouting and waving his stick at his son.

'Get out!' he raged.

'Pa...'

'Out!' Geo shouted. 'I want you gone. You bring nothing but trouble. You're not welcome in my home. You're a thief and a liar and you ruined me.'

It was Aurora who calmed things down. 'I'll take Nico outside and show him what has been done to prepare for the fire,' she suggested.

They stepped out of the small house, but there was no reprieve—Geo's words followed them out into the oppressive heat, where the air was smoky.

'He won't leave willingly,' she said.

'I know he won't.' Nico sighed.

He had his chopper waiting, and a care facility in Rome ready to receive Geo, but even as Nico had asked Marianna to put the arrangements in place he had known it was futile.

'You could carry him out,' Aurora suggested.

'I could,' Nico agreed, 'but then he would die on my shoulders just to spite me. What about you?'

'Me?'

'Yes, why are *you* staying, Aurora?'

'Because we have to protect the village.'

'And what can you do against the might of a wildfire?' Nico asked.

All five-foot-three of her. She was tiny—a stick.

Except she wasn't a stick any more.

They had avoided each other as much as possible since that awkward walk four years ago, and he had watched her blossom from a distance. The child he had rejected was now all woman. The cheeky, precocious brat who had hung on his every word was a forthright, assertive woman who, to Nico's cold surprise, completely turned him on.

Not that he showed it. For one thing had not changed.

Nico did not want a family and he did not want the responsibility of another heart.

'Aurora, you can't do anything to stop the fire.'

'I can feed the firefighters,' Aurora responded. 'Anyway, Pa says the village is safe.'

'Aurora…' Nico kept his voice even, but fear licked at his throat at the thought of her staying here.

The village was not safe. Far from it. Nico had, after all, just viewed the fires from the sky, and heard the worrying comments from his pilot, who was ex-military. Bruno, Aurora's father, was probably regretting his foolish decision and just putting on a brave face.

'Leave.'

'No.'

He persisted. 'Come with me now and get out.'

'I already told you—no.'

'I could insist…' Nico said, and it angered him when she snorted.

Did she not get that the village was going to go up in smoke and that the fire would destroy all in its path?

'I could just put you over my shoulder—the same way I am tempted to do with my father.'

'And then what, Nico? What will you do with me in Rome?'

He gritted his teeth.

'My father would not object,' she said. 'In fact, all the villagers would come out and cheer if you carried me off.' She gave him a smile that did not quite meet her eyes. 'But then you would surely return me, Nico, and that would *not* go down very well.'

No, Nico thought, it would not. 'Don't you *ever* think of leaving?' he asked.

'Why would I?' Aurora shrugged. '*La famiglia* is everything to me. Give me good food and family and my day is complete. What more could I want?'

'You should deepen your voice, Aurora,' Nico said, 'when you impersonate your father.'

'But I wasn't impersonating him.'

'No? You've heard it so often you believe it to be your own thought.'

'Why do you have to criticise?'

'I'm not.'

'Oh, but you are.'

Nico took a breath. Aurora was correct. He *was* criticising—and he had no right to. Especially when she did so much for his father.

He addressed that issue. 'You still haven't sent me your bank account details so that I can pay you for the time spent with my father.'

'I don't count it as work.'

No, she saw it as duty. Nico knew that.

Even though he had not married her, she had taken on the role of caring for his family.

'Aurora…'

'I don't have time for this, Nico. I want to move the firewood away from your father's home. I thought my brother had done it…'

'Give me a moment,' Nico said.

Walking away from the house, he took out his phone and made a call to his pilot.

He could get out.

Perhaps he even *should* get out.

As he and the pilot both agreed, it would be a waste of vital resources to have a pilot and helicopter sitting idle, just in case Geo changed his mind.

But Nico could not leave his father to his fate alone.

And neither could he leave Aurora behind.

He looked over to her, lifting logs, doing all she could to keep the old man safe.

'Right,' he said walking towards her. She was filthy from the effort and he watched the streaks of ash grow as she wiped her forehead. 'Leave the firewood to me. What else needs to be done?'

'Aren't you leaving?'

'No.'

Their conversation was interrupted with the arrival of Aurora's father. 'Nico!'

Bruno greeted him warmly, as he always did—and that consistently surprised Nico. The fact that he had refused to marry his daughter should have caused great offence, yet Bruno had confounded Nico's expectations and still treated him as a future son-in-law.

'You will stay with us,' Bruno said.

'No, no…' Nico attempted, for he did *not* want to be under the same roof as Aurora.

Or rather, he wanted to be under the same roof *alone* with Aurora. He wanted to strip her off in the shower and soap those breasts that now had sweat dripping between them.

He was trying to hold a conversation with Bruno even as filthy visions of the man's daughter flashed in his mind. What was *wrong* with him?

'So you're too good for us now?' Bruno demanded.

They all spoke from the same script, Nico thought as he dragged his mind from Aurora's breasts. To refuse Bruno's hospitality would be an insult, and although in his professional life Nico did not care who he offended, he attempted to do things differently here.

Like it or not, while his father was alive, he still needed these people.

More, though, he wanted to do the right thing.

'You can have Aurora's bed.'

'No. Absolutely not!' Nico would not hear of it.

'She will be out tonight, at Antonietta's birthday party.'

'Aurora should be at home,' Nico said. 'With the threat to the village I thought the roads would be closed.'

'The main one is, but some are open between the villages, and the threat has been here for weeks,' Bruno said. 'Life goes on, and Antonietta's father is the fire chief. The firefighters are camping on his grounds so it is the safest place for her to be.'

Nico wasn't so sure of that—and it had nothing to do with the fire!

'I could be on lookout,' Nico said, but Bruno shook his head.

'It is Pino's turn tonight. I did it last night. You shall stay with us.'

'Well, thank you for your offer, 'Nico said, 'but I shall stay only if I sleep on the sofa.'

'Up to you.' Bruno shrugged.

Before dinner Nico checked in on his father, who had drifted off into a drunken stupor. Aurora was already there, and rolling him onto his side, making sure Geo would not choke should he become unwell during the night.

'I told the store not to supply him with whisky,' Nico said to her.

'There is home delivery now.' Aurora shrugged. 'Even your father has worked out the Internet. And there's always Pino stopping by, or Francesca. You can't stop him.'

'I send money, but then I wonder...'

'If you didn't send it he would drink cheap wine instead,' Aurora pointed out. 'Come on, it's time to get back. Supper will soon be ready.'

'I need to speak with the doctor first.'

The news from the doctor was the same.

Geo needed to stop drinking and he needed a more comprehensive level of care—except there was no staff to provide it in Silibri.

'I have spoken to the agency,' Nico said to him. 'And I am looking to purchase the house across the street. That way—'

'You could purchase ten houses,' the doctor interrupted. 'No one wants to live here. The village is dying faster than your father.'

Why did Aurora choose to remain here?

Nico thought of long-ago evenings at the Messina dinner table. She would talk of her photography, and how she would pester the manager at the winery to change the labels on his wine. To rename, rebrand. She had passion and dreams—but they had been smothered by this village, like the smoke that blanketed the valley now.

'Come and sit down,' Bruno said as Nico walked into the Messina home. 'Good food and family and my day is complete. Come now, Aurora.'

But Aurora did not join them at the table.

'No, Pa, there will be food at the party and I have to get ready.'

'And will there be firemen at this party?' Bruno checked. And though he spoke to Aurora, he looked over to Nico.

'I think they are a little too busy fighting fires.' Aurora smiled sweetly as she left the room.

Nico's gut tightened.

'Aurora has a thing for one of the firefighters,' Bruno

said, and rolled his eyes. '*Per favore, mangia, mangia,* Nico. Come on—eat.'

The pasta, though delectable, tasted like ash in Nico's mouth.

Worse still, he could hear the pipes groan as Aurora turned on the shower...

It was bliss to have the hot day and all the grime slide off her skin and to feel the dirt and grease being stripped from her hair. This morning she had risen before six, and had worked every minute since, and yet though she ached, Aurora was not tired.

She looked down at her skin, brown as nutmeg, and saw her fleshy stomach and full breasts and all too solid legs.

She was too much.

Too much skin and bum and boobs.

Too much attitude.

Although as it had turned out for Nico she was not enough. Never enough for him.

How, Aurora pondered as the water drenched her, could Nico manage to turn her on even from the kitchen table?

Last week she had kissed a firefighter, and all she had felt was the tickle of his beard, and all she had tasted was the garlic on his breath, and all she had smelled was the smoke in his hair.

There was something so *clean* about Nico.

Even if his morals were filthy.

Oh, yes, she had heard the gossip about his many women!

But there was still something so clean about him— the tang of his scent and the neatness of his nails that made her shiver on the inside.

She stepped out of the shower and wrapped a towel around her body that was burning inside like the mountains that were aflame all around them.

She headed into her pink bedroom. It was too childish—she knew that—but then she should be gone by now.

Aurora thought now that she would either be the village spinster or perhaps she would marry one day.

But she would never know the bliss of Nico.

Never.

Ever.

And that made angry tears moisten her eyes.

Her nipples felt as if the surface skin had been roughened as she stuffed her breasts into her bra. And as she wrestled her dark hair into some semblance of style there was suddenly the snap of a chain, and her *collana*, the cross and chain she had worn for ever, fell to the floor.

It felt like a sign.

She felt dangerous and reckless and everything she should not be.

Oh, what was the point of being a good Italian girl when the perfect Italian boy didn't want you?

And so she went to the special book on her shelf, out of which she had cut the middle and in which hid the forbidden Pill.

The Pointless Pill, she called it, for she could not imagine sex with anyone other than Nico.

Tonight she would drink wine and try kissing that firefighter again—and maybe this time when his hand went to her breasts she would not brush him off.

To hell with you, Nico Caruso. I shall get over you.

She put blusher on her cheeks and lengthened her

lashes with mascara before sliding glossy pink onto her lips.

She dabbed perfume on her neck and wrists and then strapped on high heels. And she knew that she was not dressing for the fireman tonight, but for the one minute when she would pass Nico on her way out.

She wanted him to ache with regret.

Instead Nico ached with need when, mid-meal, Aurora teetered out in heels and a silver dress.

Nico tried not to look up.

'Go and change, Aurora,' Bruno warned.

'Why? I would just have to put my dress and shoes in a bag and change in the street,' Aurora said cheekily. 'Because I *am* wearing my silver dress tonight, whatever you say.'

Nico could not help but smile. Aurora did not hide, or lie, she just was who she was.

The taxi tooted. The one taxi that ferried people between villages.

He had to ignore the effect of her and the feeling, a lot like fear, that rose when he thought of her out on those fiery mountains tonight.

As she bent and kissed her father, her mother, her brother, he found he had to stop himself from running a tense hand down his jaw and neck as he awaited the torture to come.

Torture for them both.

If she did not extend to him the traditional farewell it would give rise to comments. Her omission would be noted and it would be awkward indeed.

He sat at the head of the table, and as she bent she put her hand on its surface to make as little contact with Nico as she could.

His cheek was cool when her lips brushed it. His scent she tried to obliterate by not breathing in. But because her brother leaned forward to ladle out more pasta she had to move quickly and put out a hand on Nico's shoulder.

It was solid and warm.

One cheek to go.

Both were holding their breath.

Their desire was like the cattails and the bulrushes, waiting to be snapped open and for a million seeds to fly out and expand.

'Be safe,' he told her, in a voice that was somewhat gruff.

She gave the tiniest unreadable smile, and in it was a glint of danger as she straightened up.

'I'm not your problem, Nico.'

She was, Nico knew, looking for trouble tonight.

Hell.

CHAPTER FOUR

Later on the night that neither can forget...

'WE SHOULD HAVE got out.'

Aurora turned and looked at Antonietta as the three friends sat on the hillside, watching the ominous glow.

'We'll make it,' Chi-Chi said. 'There is soon to be a storm.'

'And with storms come lightning,' Antonietta pointed out. 'I wish I had left. I wish I had taken off to...' She thought for a moment. 'Paris.'

'But you don't speak French,' Aurora said.

'I'm learning it.' Antonietta shrugged, and then was silent for another moment before continuing. 'Pa says we shall have a proper party after the fires. I'm getting engaged.'

Chi-Chi let out a squeal and jumped up in excitement.

'To Sylvester,' Antonietta added, and she looked to Aurora, who had to fight not to pull a face.

For Antonietta and Sylvester were second cousins, and Aurora was sure this was a match to keep money within the family rather than for love.

'Are you happy?' Aurora asked carefully.

Antonietta was silent for a very long time, and then she shrugged an odd response. *'C'est la vie!'*

Aurora didn't really know what that meant, but she could hear the weary resignation in her friend's voice and it troubled her.

'I hear your Nico is back,' Antonietta said.

'He is not *my* Nico,' Aurora said.

'No,' Chi-Chi agreed, and made a scoffing noise. 'You should forget about him,' she said. And then she nudged her as a fire truck turned into the hillside, bringing weary firefighters for a break, some food, and maybe a kiss…

But Antonietta caught Aurora's arm. 'If Nico is back, then what are you doing here?'

'He doesn't want me,' Aurora said.

But Antonietta, though only newly twenty-one, had an old head on her young shoulders.

'Go home,' Antonietta said. 'Fix what you can, while you still can. I heard my father speaking to his men about the direction of the fire…'

And hearing the solemn note in Antonietta's voice, and watching the weary firefighters approach, Aurora no longer wanted to be out in the valley tonight.

This… Nico thought as he sat at the table with Aurora's parents playing cards. *This would have been my life.*

Hard work out on the vines by day, and a tired body at night.

Except no amount of labour would be enough to tire his mind.

Yet, on the plus side, he would be sitting with Aurora in the now vacant house across the road, rather than looking at Bruno's hairy arms as he shuffled the cards.

Just because Nico did not want to be married to Aurora, and just because Nico did not want to stay, it did not mean there was not desire. It did not mean he did not care.

And he *loathed* the thought of her out there tonight.

'I'm going to check on my father,' Nico said.

He found Geo deeply asleep, and as he came out Nico felt the hot winds lick his face. He looked at the glowing mountains, and the approaching fire spreading towards them, and in the distance he could see lightning strikes.

They were sitting ducks, Nico thought as he went back into the Messina house.

'Bruno, can I borrow your car and go and get Aurora? The fire is moving fast...'

But Aurora's work-shy brother had just taken it, Bruno said. 'And anyway, Aurora will not thank you if you interfere with her plans for tonight. I've told you she is in the safest place. They're not going to let the chief firefighter's house burn.'

Dio! Nico wanted to shout. *Do you really think the fire will give them a choice?*

'If it gets much closer,' Bruno continued, 'Aurora knows to come home and we will head to the beach.'

He wanted to shake Bruno and ask, *Is it not better that we all die together?* But then, he did not want to worry her mother.

'Grab a cushion from Aurora's room,' Bruno said, 'You know where it is.'

Oh, he knew.

The scent of Aurora lingered in the air. He looked down and saw her gold cross on the floorboards. He picked it up and held it in his palm for a moment.

He caught sight of the book on her chest of drawers and he was intrigued, because he knew that poetry was not her thing. Even before he opened it Nico almost knew what he would see.

The little packet of pills, half of them gone, had been left for him to see, Nico was sure.

He replaced the book in her top drawer.

Message received, Aurora. Loud and clear.

And tonight it was killing him.

The sofa was soft.

Nico was not.

He heard the taxi drop some people off in the street, followed by some chatter—but not Aurora's throaty voice.

The taxi service stopped at midnight.

It was ten past midnight now.

He thumped the cushion and put it over his head to block out the sound of Bruno's snores.

Signora Messina must have had enough, because she shouted for her husband to be quiet and for a short while silence reigned. Except for the drone of the firebombers, filling up in the ocean and then heading back to the hills.

Then, deep in the night, he heard the baker's truck rattle past and stop. He knew that truck was the last chance to get home, for he had taken it many times—except in his case Nico would often leave Silibri in it, heading to the next village.

Anything to get away.

He ached from his calves to his groin to hear Aurora's footsteps. From the small of his back to his chest, need gripped him tightly and fear for her choked him.

And then the door opened quietly, and Nico breathed a sigh of relief when he heard the pad of bare feet and guessed that she was carrying her shoes.

Aurora tiptoed past him.

She couldn't really see him on the sofa—it was more she could feel that he was there.

She was so sick of Nico and his effect on her that it was all she could do not to spit in his direction.

Instead, she crept into the bathroom and stared at her streaked mascara and wild hair for a moment before she brushed her teeth.

She couldn't even kiss anyone else.

The fireman was quite attractive.

Big and bearded, he was the type of man who would get on with her father. He lived in the next village and had said he was more than happy to come and meet her family, if that was what it took to get to know Aurora some more.

He was perfectly nice—but he was not Nico.

In every dream, in every thought, it was Nico she kissed, Nico who was her first, and she did not know how to change the grooves in which her mind was stuck.

Nico's hands on her body.

Nico's mouth on hers.

She washed her face, stripped off her clothes and pulled on a baggy old T-shirt that had seen better days.

But instead of heading to her bedroom it was the kitchen to which she headed, her choice fully made.

Nico *would* be her first.

He heard the fridge door open and water being poured, but feigned sleep as she stood over him.

'I know you're awake,' Aurora said.

'How come you're back?'

She didn't answer.

'What have you been doing?'

'I don't answer to you,' Aurora said, and then shrugged. 'I was just sitting on the hillside, talking…'

'With?'

'You forfeited any right to ask, Nico.'

'With?' he asked again.

'Chi-Chi and Antonietta.'

'And your firefighter?'

'He wants me. You don't.'

'So why are you here?'

'I don't want him. I want you.'

Nico could hear her despair and he took her hand, pulled her a little towards him, indicating for her to sit down.

'Aurora,' he said. 'Me not wanting to marry has nothing to do with you.'

'I would say it has *everything* to do with me, given our fathers agreed—'

'Since when did I *ever* do as my father wished?' Nico interrupted.

'You rejected me.'

'You were *sixteen*—and if you want to take offence that I was not attracted to some teenager who I looked at as a sister, then that is your choice.'

Aurora swallowed. She had never thought of it like that.

'You think of me as a sister?'

'I did.'

And now he did not.

'Do you think of me the same way now? Or as a friend?' she asked.

'We can never be friends Aurora.'

Some might take that as an insult, Aurora thought, but it was true. She did not want to do the things she wanted to do to Nico with her friends.

'What have you been doing?' he asked again.

'Trying to fit in—but as always I didn't.'

'What do you mean?'

'Chi-Chi is desperate to marry and Antonietta…' She hesitated, and then told Nico what he might not know, as it was very recent news. 'She is soon to be engaged to Sylvester.'

'But isn't he her cousin?'

'Second cousin, I think,' Aurora said, and watched as Nico pulled a slight face. 'I don't think she's happy about it.'

'I can't say I blame her.'

Nico sighed. If Aurora was fire, then Antonietta was ice, and did not show her feelings. If Aurora thought Antonietta unhappy, then she was.

'So,' Aurora continued. 'There is Chi-Chi wanting a husband, Antonietta not wanting one, and as for me…' She took a breath and told him, 'I am twenty and only last week had my first kiss.'

'Just a kiss?' Nico asked, and she nodded.

'I hated it,' she admitted.

Nico wasn't sure he believed her. 'You need to hide your Pill better, Aurora.'

'You were snooping?'

'And you think your parents don't?' said Nico.

'Usually I'm more careful. I was in a rush tonight.'

'So, if you have just had your first kiss, and hated it, why are you on the Pill?'

'If you build it they will come,' Aurora said. 'Or hopefully *I* will.'

He laughed.

So did she.

Oh, they laughed—and it was such a moment, such a shared flash of bliss, to see cold, immutable Nico lie there and laugh, that she did what she knew she should not and moved her hand to his cheek.

His hand went to remove it, but instead it held hers there.

'It's me who doesn't fit in, Aurora. I don't want relationships. I don't want responsibilities.'

'And you probably don't want someone who can't kiss.'

'Aurora, trust me—you can kiss.'

'Can I try it on you?'

'No.'

'I repulse you so much?'

'You know you don't.'

'Then why not let me kiss you?'

'I'm not your practice board.'

'So I go back to my firefighter…' Aurora said, and felt his hands grip her fingers tighter.

'One kiss.'

He said it with authority, but the undercurrent suggested they both hoped he was lying.

How to kiss him? Aurora pondered. How best to claim her one kiss?

'What are you doing?' Nico asked.

'I want to see you,' Aurora said, and she climbed up so she sat on his stomach, and it made her insides melt that he helped her *and* that he smiled.

She had not looked at her firefighter. In fact she had closed her eyes—though not in bliss.

Now she looked.

His face was still beautiful in the dark: the shadows in the hollows of his cheeks, the dent in his strong jaw, and those delectable lips, and those black eyes watching her.

'You know how to kiss, Aurora,' he told her, and she lowered her head to his.

She felt the softness of his mouth, and his pleasurably rough jaw, and she lingered there for a moment, lightly kissing his full lips.

He had *such* a nice mouth.

She gave that nice mouth playful kisses that teased, that were almost friendly—but not chaste. It was like a little warm-up…like poking a big, sleeping bear.

She could feel his naked torso between her legs and the warmth of his belly on her sex as she practised her kiss on him.

'Taste me with your tongue,' he told her, and she saw that Nico's eyes were now closed.

'I'm too shy.'

That elicited another laugh from them both. It was nice to laugh as their mouths mingled, to share in each other's breath—and then his hand came behind her head and Aurora received her first proper kiss, for with one sweep of his tongue he discounted all the others.

Finally, she closed her eyes.

Then, as he sucked her tongue and pressed her head into his, she knew she was right to be there, for her body was on fire for him.

He tasted of *limoncello* and water and skill. He gave her a taste of the passion beneath that aloof exterior and he made her crave him.

She rose on her haunches and his other hand came to her waist as he kissed her more deeply, tangling with her in indecent ways. His hand slipped down to her buttocks—and he pulled his head away.

'*Dio*, Aurora, where are your knickers?'

'I don't wear them to bed.' She smiled. 'It's too hot.'

His hands were on her ripe flesh and she could feel his fingers digging hard into her. And then she recognised the reluctance in him and felt regret as he removed them.

'Do you wear *your* underwear to bed?' she asked.

She slid back and sat on his thighs. It was a very provocative move, for in doing so she slid her naked sex over the hardest part of him. She pulled back the cot-

ton blanket and saw beneath his black silk boxers and
the clear evidence of his desire for her.

'Oh, Nico...'

She touched him without fear or hesitation, freeing
him from the restraint that had kept their actions decent.
She explored him with her eyes and her hands and knew
she had never seen anything more beautiful in her life.

'Aurora...' he warned, and removed her hand, or
soon he wouldn't be able to control himself any more.

But she did not stop, and when her hand returned
he did not halt it.

'Make it stop, Nico,' she begged.

'Make what stop?'

'This *fire*.'

'Go to bed,' he told her, pushing at her hips and attempting to lift her from his thighs.

But she dug in. 'No.'

'Okay,' he compromised. 'I'll make you come, and
then you are to go to bed.'

His arrogant tone only turned her on even more, and
she relished the opportunity to discover what he could
make her body feel.

Oh, he brought bliss with his fingers. He was not
gentle, and she stifled a cry as he slipped his fingers
inside her. She moved with his hand for a moment, but
then sobbed in frustration. 'It's not your hand I want...'

'Let go,' he told her as he stroked her more insis-
tently, increasing the speed and pressure of his fingers
according to the responses of her body.

When she climaxed, Nico decided, he would allow
himself to join her, and then they could both get some
sleep.

'We might be going to die tonight, Nico,' she told
him. 'Don't let me die a virgin.'

She looked down at him and felt a shiver rippling inside her as he almost smiled.

But *was* it a smile?

Aurora did not know, for it was a look she had never before seen. It was a kind of grim smile that made her stomach flip, and his voice, when it came, was deeper than thunder, with a low warning edge.

'Get on the floor,' he told her.

'No,' she said. For that would mean separating their bodies and she did not want to give him even a second to change his mind.

That grim smile remained as his hand left her sex and moved to his own. 'Take off your top,' he told her. 'I want to know every inch of you.'

With anticipation bubbling inside her, and delight that she was finally getting her way, she pulled her T-shirt over her head.

Aurora put her hands on his chest and lifted herself a little. She looked down as he held himself in one hand and ran the glistening tip against her most sensitive flesh.

'Don't make a noise,' he warned as he nudged against her, except she was too tight for his thick length.

He could feel her thighs shaking as she knelt up. 'Get on the floor,' he said again, for he could better control things there.

'Please, Nico, *now*!'

He was just a little way inside her, and he took her hips in his large palms. He'd meant to do it more gently, but she was damp with perspiration, and so was he, and as he pushed her down their bodies slid together and he pulled her down harder than he'd intended and seared into her virgin flesh.

It was the most painful, exquisite, blissful moment

of her life and she did not make a sound. It was Nico who let out a breathless cry as he took her virginity.

'Shh…' Aurora said, though the sound stroked through her as they locked together. She stayed still, so still, because it was agony, but it was delicious too, and she felt his hands very gently on her hips, steadying her.

'Come here,' he told her, but did not move an inch. 'Let me kiss you.'

Now he made her moan, for his kiss was her first taste of the true Nico—utterly tender and all man. His kiss and his tongue took all the hurt away as his hands stroked her hips—not to move her, just to feel her—and he made her whimper. And as the hurt receded desire took its place and she started to move according to the demands of her own body.

She wanted to linger on his lips, to savour this side of Nico, but her body wouldn't allow it, for she could not kiss him softly *and* move as she wished to at the same time.

Nico took over, holding her hips and bringing her in line with his building rhythm, lifting his hips to thrust into her.

'Nico…' she said, in a voice that was fighting not to scream. 'Nico…'

He wasn't putting out the fire in her—it was spreading and consuming her, and she did not recognise the approaching bliss, but sought it all the same.

And then he let out that breathless shout again and lifted himself.

Feeling Nico swell and then the rush of his relief fill her, caused Aurora to shatter into a thousand tiny pieces. And Nico, *her* Nico, pressed his hand over her mouth as her world went black and her orgasm coursed through her.

It was the most intense moment she had ever known and he guided her through it.

Aurora started kissing his palm. Kissing and tasting his salty skin. His hand slid behind her head and he pulled her back to his kiss.

They came down from their high together and slowly. Back to the world they had left for a while. Back to the sound of the choppers and her father's snores.

He held her for a while, but he was concerned about the pace and direction of the fire, and soon he went to the window and checked the solid red glow on the hillside.

And then he looked back to the sofa, where Aurora lay...

Aurora knew she must return to her bed.

'Come on,' Nico said, and took her hand.

He helped her up, and as Aurora stood on shaky legs she fought the sting of tears. How could he be so close one moment and then pack her off to bed like a child the next?

He picked up her T-shirt and led her through to the small kitchen. He turned on the light and she looked down and saw blood, and the evidence of their coupling.

'I can't have a shower—they'll hear the pipes.'

'I know,' Nico said.

Instead he turned on the water at the sink and began to wash her, slowly and carefully.

Tenderly.

It was the second best moment of her life.

Then he put the T-shirt over her head. She did not get another kiss, but he held her for a moment and then released her.

Aurora returned to her pink bedroom and lay in a bed in which she no longer felt she belonged.

CHAPTER FIVE

AURORA AWOKE VERY EARLY, as she always did, in her own bed, but to a world that felt different.

She gave no thought to the wildfires.

For days she had been obsessed by them, but now her first thoughts were of Nico and what had happened between them.

There was no regret—in fact it was bliss to recall. But there was a tremble of fear. For she had not thought she could love him more, or want him more, than she had this time yesterday.

But she did.

Only then did she register the sound of rain—a light patter against her window. Aurora climbed out of bed and peered out. There was steam from the heat, and black smoke in the sky, and a steady fine drizzle of rain.

Aurora pulled on a dress and sandals, and as she slipped out of the house she stole just one look at Nico, crashed out on the couch.

Nico was not feigning sleep this time, but he woke at the sound of the door closing softly and then the steady, welcome patter of rain.

He was not one to examine his emotions—more often he shut them down—but for a moment he lay there, trying to label how he felt.

It wasn't so much regret that had him closing his eyes tight, for in all his twenty-six years those hours last night had been the best of his life.

It was guilt.

Guilt because although everything had changed between them nothing had changed about what he wanted from his life. He did not want love and he certainly didn't want marriage.

Nico had lost control in the small hours and he was not used to losing control.

He always used condoms.

Always.

Yet last night he had not given them so much as a thought.

Had her brother come home, or if her parents had got up and caught them, they would be heading over to the priest right now to arrange a wedding.

Instead he dressed, and headed out to where he knew he would find her.

It was muggy and humid, and no doubt the water would evaporate long before it got to the fires, but the rain would certainly help because the mountains had been tinder-dry.

Down through the village he headed, towards the cliffs overlooking the ocean.

He found her walking through the temple ruins, clearly deep in thought, because she jumped a little when she saw him, evidently not having heard his approach.

'Are you okay?' Nico asked.

'Of course,' Aurora said.

She knew she must look a sight, with her damp dress and hair, but there was nothing she could do about that.

Nico's shirt was damp too, and his black hair was

wet from the rain. She guessed this was what he would look like coming out of the shower, and thought of the shower they hadn't been able to have last night.

'Do you have any regrets?' Nico asked.

'About last night?' Aurora checked. 'None.'

She wouldn't change it even if she could. The things Aurora would change would be the now and the future without him.

'Do you?'

'In part,' Nico admitted, 'because I loathe mixed messages and—'

'I get the message, Nico,' Aurora halted him. 'I heard it loud and clear—you don't want to marry me and—'

'I don't want to marry, *period*,' Nico said. 'I don't ever want a relationship.'

And therein lay the difference between them, thought Aurora. How did he so easily separate sex from a relationship? For she felt as if she was in a relationship with Nico. Right now, as they walked through the ruins, she felt the closest she ever had to another soul.

'Aurora, you don't want to be married to me.'

Yes, Aurora did. But for dignity's sake she had to sound as if she wasn't imploding when she spoke, and so she took a breath.

'No, I don't,' she said. 'I don't want to be married to a man whose skin crawls at the thought of being here. I don't want to be married to a man who keeps his hand on my shoulder but his eyes on the pretty—'

'What are you *talking* about?'

Aurora just shrugged, and then asked him a question. 'When are you leaving?'

'I'll see what's happening with the fires,' Nico said, 'but I expect I shall leave today.'

Even the heavens were against her, Aurora decided,

because as he said it the drizzle turned into heavy rain. Yes, he would be leaving today.

'Aurora, did you think last night might change things?'

'No.'

She had been under no illusion that having sex with Nico would change anything for him. There had been a kernel of hope, though…

And Nico crushed it.

'I'll never marry, Aurora.'

'I shall,' she said, and she said it harshly.

Her words punished Nico, but determinedly he did not let it show. 'You have your own life to live and you have no obligation to me.'

'I know.'

'So, please, if you are going to help care for my father, at least give me your bank details.'

'I don't want your dirty money.'

'*Dirty* money?'

'Oh, come on, Nico, don't take me for a fool. Since when did a boy from Silibri leave school at sixteen and go on to own hotels and his own helicopter?'

'You really are good at assuming the worst, aren't you, Aurora?'

'What else is there to think?' She stopped walking then and looked at him. 'Nico, be careful.'

'Of what?'

'Whatever it is you're mixed up in.'

'You think I'm in the mafia?' Nico said. 'Or moving drugs?' He *loathed* that she thought that of him. 'I'm not involved in anything like that.'

'Come off it, Nico,' Aurora said, and tried to walk off. 'Don't lie to me.'

He caught her arm. 'I'm not,' Nico said, he was

angry. 'Please don't take me for some corrupt mafia gangster.'

'I don't,' Aurora said. 'Or I'm trying not to.'

'Aurora, ask and I'll tell you—but only you.'

She stood in the rain and it *still* felt like a relationship. She should walk away now, not draw herself in closer to a man who would never want her completely.

She asked, 'How?'

'You know when I left here that I went to my grandfather's?'

Aurora nodded. 'On your mother's side?'

'*Sì.* They are very modest people, who never cared much for my father. They thought my mother had made a poor choice, but she ran off and married him anyway. My grandfather suggested that I cut all ties with my father, but I could not. I got a job there and I sent half my wage home to him. I knew that he was not well and could no longer work the vines—'

'He could have,' Aurora interrupted. 'He chose not to.'

'Perhaps,' Nico conceded. 'Anyway, I made my own way. I worked in a bar, and then I took a loan, and then I bought a small stake in the bar and put in more hours.'

'That does *not* buy you a five-star hotel in Rome and three others.'

'I don't *own* four hotels, Aurora. I have stakes in them.'

She shook her head, disbelieving. No, a Sicilian woman could not be beguiled.

'What I *do* own,' Nico said, 'is land.'

He looked to the misty grey waters and the cliffs shining from the rain.

'This will go no further?' he checked.

'Of course.'

'Even when you sit on the hill drinking wine with Antonietta?'

'She won't be hearing about last night, Nico.'

'This might be a more difficult secret to keep.'

He smiled at her slight eyebrow-raise, and the fact was he *wanted* to tell her. Nico wanted her take on the decision he was about to make.

'My father married my mother not for love, but for what he thought he would get.'

'Which was…?'

He led her out of the temple ruins and they walked towards the old monastery.

'My grandfather owned the land we stand on—right to the edge of the temple ruins. When my mother died, he said the only good that could come out of it was that my father would never get his hands on it. He left it to me. That is why my father says I stole from him.'

'Why did he want it?' Aurora said.

She did not doubt it was beautiful—and, yes, the view was divine—but as far as she could see it was worthless, and she told him so.

'Houses sit empty here for years. My father goes on about the house he had for—' She swallowed, not wanting to say 'us' when no such thing existed. 'He could not even give it away.' She looked around again. Yes, it was her playground and, yes, she loved it, but… 'There's just the carcass of the old monastery and those steps down to the beach.'

'It's *gold*, Aurora. And my father would have sold it to developers. We would be standing now in a concrete jungle, with tourists being bussed in from the airport every day.'

Aurora could not picture it, though she tried to. 'It

would be good for the village, though, to have people coming through…'

'In some ways it would—but that is not what my grandfather wanted and I agreed with him. He thought the monastery should be restored, but that would mean bringing stone up from the quarries…' He halted. The cost and logistics were appalling. 'Believe me, I have been tempted to just sell it—'

'No!' Aurora cried, and it was emphatic. 'He left it to you!'

'Yes.' Nico nodded. 'But I didn't even know he owned it until a short while before he died.'

'Yet you spoke of his plans for it?'

'I thought they were just nostalgic ramblings about his hometown,' Nico admitted. 'And my father certainly never told me about it—though when I found out I understood better why he hates me so. He married my mother to get his hands on it.'

Aurora looked at the land she loved and knew so well, but she looked with different eyes now. It was Nico's.

'What will you do with it?'

'I don't have to do anything. It's a huge asset and I can keep building on that.'

'Or sell it to developers?'

'No,' Nico said, for he had ruled that option out long ago, even if at times he'd been tempted. And then he said what had long been on his mind. 'I could restore the monastery.'

'And make it into what?'

'A very exclusive, very luxurious hotel.'

Aurora swallowed.

'Just a few suites…'

'But how would that make a profit?'

'I would charge a fortune to stay in my Silibri hotel, and I believe I would get it.'

Aurora heard the steely resolve in his voice and blinked, because businessman Nico was someone she did not know.

She spoke then. 'It would bring people back to Silibri…'

'It would,' Nico said, and then he made sure he crushed that last kernel of hope. 'But not me. At least not permanently.'

'I get it, Nico.'

She did.

Nico would not be returning to Silibri to live.

He looked at the ruins, and then he looked to the shell of an old stone cottage, and vowed it would be the first thing that was restored. Yes, he would be back to see his father, but there would be no reason to spend another night in the Messina house.

Nico would not do that to Aurora.

And finally, after years of indecision over the land, his decision was made.

He would not marry Aurora.

But he would take care of her this way.

CHAPTER SIX

Rome

THE LAST TEAR.

It spilled out as she began to pull herself together.

Enough.

She swore there and then that it would be the last tear she shed over Nico Caruso.

Aurora wiped it from her cheek and crumpled the sodden tissue in disgust.

Alone in her hotel room, with the others on the bus tour, she was bent double with the strength of her tears as she relived that night and the morning after.

Well, she had relived it for the last time and she had embarrassed herself enough over him.

It really was time to move on.

So, instead of peeling another tissue from the box she topped up her lip-gloss over swollen lips and tried to repair the damage her crying binge had caused to her eyes.

She would not sit in her hotel room and mourn him—or rather mourn the fantasy of him—for a moment longer.

It was springtime in Rome.

She downloaded that dating app and scrolled through

it, but when she tried to write her profile she gave in and thought, *Baby steps, Aurora.*

She headed down to the bar, more than a little nervous about walking in alone.

And just as she was doing her best to get over Nico, who did she see walking towards her?

A scowling Nico, who, from his expression, wasn't expecting to see her either.

'Aurora.' He gave a swift nod.

'Buona sera.' It took everything she had to greet him with a smile.

'Buona sera. I thought you were on a bus trip?'

'No.' She did not elaborate 'I'm going to have a drink at the bar.'

'Alone?' Nico frowned.

'Not for long hopefully!' She smiled at her own little joke. 'I'll see you tomorrow.' Then she corrected herself. 'Oh, no, I won't. You're heading home in the morning.'

'Here is my home, Aurora.'

'Ah, but home is where the heart is, Nico. You know that.'

'I do,' he agreed. 'And I shall say it again—here is my home.'

He ordered his head to give her a nod and his legs to turn and walk off, but neither obeyed. And then, even as his common sense was screaming at him to walk away, he spoke. 'And, given you are in my hometown, let me get you a drink.'

He'd done it again.

Just when she was determined to move on from him he pulled her back to him.

Well, not this time, Aurora told herself. Yes, she would have a drink with him, but she would not be making a fool of herself again.

He was her boss and she would hold on to that fact.

The bar was busy and he put a hand on her upper arm to guide her through. Staff jumped into action and they were taken to a quiet corner table.

'It's so busy I thought I'd have to drink at the bar,' Aurora said. Although that was possibly the reason he had joined her. 'It's lucky we got a table.' That sounded naïve. 'I mean, I'm glad no one was asked to move to make way for the boss.'

'It would be poor form to do that to my guests, which is why this table is reserved solely for me.'

He watched as her lips pursed and wondered what he could possibly have said to upset her, for it looked as if she was tempted to get up and walk out.

Aurora was.

His private table did not impress her. In fact she felt a little insulted as she wondered how many other women had sat in this very seat. How many hands had he held across this very table?' And then she halted herself, for Nico was the last person she could imagine being affectionate.

They ordered their drinks—a spritzer for Aurora and a red wine for Nico—and then sat in tense silence as they waited for them to arrive.

'Aren't you going to ask me how your father is?' Aurora asked.

'I spoke with him two hours ago and I see his doctor tomorrow.'

'My mother is taking in his meals while I'm away. In case you were wondering.'

Nico said nothing and Aurora took a deep breath, trying to keep her exasperation in. Reminding herself that Nico did not want to hear anything about home...

She was supposed to be keeping things professional,

Aurora told herself. Except his father was fading. Did Nico properly know that?

'Look, Nico, I know that after all he did to you, you must hate him, but I think—'

'I don't,' Nico interrupted. 'I love him very much.'

For Aurora the sky turned purple, the floor was now sand and the people in the bar were green.

Everything she knew was gone.

'I have to accept, though, that he does not want my love. Still, tomorrow I will try again, and I will be told to get lost again.'

Their drinks were brought to them and even after Aurora had taken a sip of hers the revelation had not sunk in.

'You *love* him?'

'Always.'

His response was made in a voice she had never heard. One she did not know how to describe, for it was both decided and resigned.

'So, no,' Nico continued, 'I will *not* ask you how my father is, because I am in touch with his doctor every day. I know he is failing. I have sent him the lifting chair that you texted me about. And I have a chef in Palermo currently trying to recreate some dinner he keeps speaking about. One that his mother once made. I hope that it will prompt him to eat.'

'Nico…'

She did not know what to say. Oh, the hell of loving someone who beat you! The hell of loving someone who goaded and taunted you.

'He seems a little happier,' she said, and saw his disbelieving look. But she spoke the truth. 'He seems calmer,' she told him. 'Although I have a confession, Nico. I was a very bad carer and bought him some whisky last week. We watched a television show together and we laughed…'

'Thank you,' Nico said.

Aurora resisted reaching over and taking his hand. Nico did not like affection, but she ached to give it to him. She attempted to keep some distance, as she told him the painful truth. 'He's nearing the end.'

'I know he is.'

Aurora felt selfish for her assumption that Nico was going home just to avoid her. She sensed he had closed the subject, and so, after a moment's pensive silence between them, she looked around the lavish bar.

'Pino will be upset he missed this,' Aurora said. 'He wanted to buy you a drink and a meal.'

'He wanted me to go on the bus tour.'

That made Aurora laugh.

'I'm meeting them all for breakfast tomorrow, before I fly off.'

'I wasn't told.'

'There's an invitation being delivered to your rooms at turndown,' Nico said. 'And before you tell me that I should not be so formal with old friends, I will explain *again* that this trip is not about friends visiting Rome. It is work—and I take my work very seriously.'

'I know,' Aurora said. 'And so do your staff. But aside from that fact, we *are* friends visiting Rome.'

He said nothing.

'Well, *they* are your friends,' she amended, for Nico had once told Aurora that they could never be friends. 'Whether you want them to be or not.'

Nico's eyes shuttered, and he wished that it was enough to obliterate the knives of her words—for she was right. Pino *et al* were his friends.

More than friends.

It takes a village...

And it was true that the people of Silibri had raised him.

He had sat in the park as a terrified child and Bruno Messina had insisted he come back to their home to sleep.

And he had been so hungry at times, too proud to beg, but the emptier his cupboards the more frequent the invitations.

'Hey, Nico!' Pino would say. 'I need some work done in my yard.'

And that had meant supper...

'Nico,' Francesca would say. 'I have made too many *biscotti*. Take them before they go stale.'

Tomorrow, at breakfast, he would take off his jacket and he would smile and laugh with them. Somehow, before the hotel opened and it was all down to business, he would thank the people who had always been there.

'Don't you ever wonder about home?' Aurora asked.

'I hear enough of what's going on,' Nico said. He didn't like invasive gossip and exaggerated stories, but then he looked at Aurora. 'Yes.'

They shared a small smile.

'How's Chi-Chi?' he asked.

'Still looking for a husband.'

'Do you ever hear from Antonietta?'

'Occasionally.' Aurora nodded, but then she shook her head. 'Not as much as I would like. I miss her a lot.'

'You were close,' he agreed.

'Yes.'

'I *would* like to know what happened at The Wedding that Never Was.'

'You heard about that?' Aurora checked.

'Everyone who has a drop of Sicilian blood probably did!'

Aurora gave a small smile and took a sip of her drink, but she didn't lean forward in glee and share the details with him. He knew Aurora hurt for her friend.

'We just sat there in the church…waiting,' she told him. 'Waiting and waiting for the bride to arrive.'

'Did you have any clue that Antonietta wasn't going to show up?'

'No.'

'Aurora…?' he checked.

'It's the truth, Nico. I guessed she wasn't happy, but I knew no more than I told you that night—'

Whoops! They were trying not to refer to that.

'I was surprised and a bit hurt that she didn't ask me to be her bridesmaid. And I knew she wasn't thrilled at the idea of marrying Sylvester, but her father is so forceful. Both families are.'

'And so you sat in the church and you waited…?' Nico prompted.

'Yes. A car arrived, and then word spread that it was not the bride—just Antonietta's father. The priest spoke to him outside.'

'And…?'

'A fight broke out in the church. It was terrible, Nico. As soon as I worked out what was happening I left and got a ride up to her parents' house, but Antonietta was already on the *cuccette* to France.'

'She took the train out?'

Aurora nodded. 'I miss her very much, but she will never be back. She wrote and told me, but I knew it already—for how *can* she come back? Her name is mud all through the village and beyond. Not with her friends, but she has a very large family.'

Nico would have liked to tell her that time would

heal things, but he knew only too well how people could hold a grudge.

'Anyway,' Aurora said, 'I've decided that I'm going to go and see her.'

'In France?'

She nodded. 'As soon as I've saved up enough and have some leave owing I'm going to book my flight.'

He wanted to point out that she'd already have enough money if she would just let him pay her for his father's care. Nico really wanted her to have that holiday with her friend in France, but he'd have to work out a way to give it to her. Without offending her, of course. Or misleading her.

'Do you want another drink?' Nico offered. 'Or perhaps we could get dinner.'

'You told me to step out of your shadow, Nico,' Aurora said. 'You told me that I was here for work. We've caught up on family and friends, so let's just keep it about business.' Aurora was proud of herself for that, at least.

'Okay. Tell me about this idea you have.'

'I thought you didn't deal with assistants?' Aurora sneered, reminding herself of how appalling his treatment of her today had been. 'I'm going to speak with Vincenzo tomorrow. I will give *him* my idea and watch as he gets promoted.'

He smiled.

It was the most dangerous thing, for she could feel her resolve melting like the ice cubes at the bottom of her glass.

'Tell *me*, Aurora.'

'No.' But she was so excited that she couldn't *not* share it. 'Okay—I think we should offer a very exclusive package for weddings at the temple ruins.'

'I don't own that land.'

'But you own the land that surrounds it, and without that access it's very difficult to get to.'

'Yes, but there might be tourists about, or—'

'Nico, it will be the same as a beach wedding. Of course there might be tourists or people walking there. And,' she went on, 'I know that whatever we come up with it might have to change later—there might one day be ten hotels in Silibri—'

'Not like mine.' Nico gave an adamant shake of his head.

The monastery had been a hellish restoration, and no developer in their right mind would have gone to the lengths he had. That aside, there was nowhere else with the views from the old monastery, nowhere with such access.

'Aurora, it would be...' He was about to put up obstacles, and there were many, but she was right. He knew that, for of course *he* had considered it. 'It would be brilliant—'

'But only in the right hands,' Aurora said. 'Only with the right manager.'

'We have a functions manager.'

'I'd want to make weddings at the temple separate. Exclusive,' Aurora said. 'And I want that role.'

'You have no experience,' Nico pointed out. 'You have been in the hospitality industry for four weeks. Before that—'

'I was a cleaner—and a very good one,' Aurora said. 'Is your father's house not spotless?'

'It is.'

Aurora had just combined three of his least favourite topics—his father, the fact that she was his father's unpaid help, and weddings.

'And I have contacts,' she said. 'I know everyone…'

'Aurora…' He kept his voice even. 'It's a good idea—an excellent one. But let's get the hotel up and running first.'

She could not wait, though. 'Nico, we could have wedding gowns for hire, for couples who want to be spontaneous. I *want* this to happen. I *want* that role and I will tell you why. I *know* what the temple looks like in the early morning, and in summer and in winter. I *know* how it looks when the moon is low at night…' To prove it she took out her phone and moved her chair round the table so she sat next to him. 'Look!'

With the scent of her close, with her bare arm next to his suited one, with her voice so close he could *feel* its vibration, Nico decided it was safer indeed to look at the images on her phone.

And they really were breathtaking.

'Since I could walk I have explored those ruins almost daily. For years I have—'

It was she who halted now, for she could not reveal to Nico that it was there she had envisaged their wedding. Not in the tiny little village church, but there at the temple ruins.

It had been a pointless dream—she had known even then—for her parents would never have agreed to her marrying anywhere other than in church.

She felt his arm against hers and the heat from his thigh—or was it from hers? They were sitting so close to each other, and it had happened so naturally, but she felt terribly aware of that fact.

She moved herself and her chair to a far safer location.

Opposite him.

'At least think about it,' Aurora said. 'And think of

me...' She paused and their eyes met across the table. 'I mean, consider me for the role.'

'Of course,' Nico said, and still his eyes held hers. 'And I *do* think of you, Aurora.'

She did not know what to say to that. She felt the pull of him, but it was all too late, she decided. She had put him behind her.

She tore her eyes from his gaze and looked down to her glass, which was empty.

'Another one?' Nico said.

'I had better get on,' Aurora said. She stood and put her bag over her shoulder. 'Thank you for the drink, Nico. It was good to catch up.'

He walked her out and towards the elevators, and she could feel the thick energy between them. She dreaded that he might kiss her—but only because it would take a stronger woman than her to say no.

'You had better go,' Aurora said. 'You have an early start. I know because I booked your driver.'

'I *should* go,' Nico agreed.

In fact, Aurora was the very reason he wasn't staying at the hotel that night—to avoid just such a situation as this. And yet even with all his exit strategies planned here they stood, face to face.

'I will see you at breakfast before I leave?'

'I await my invitation,' Aurora said.

'It will be on your pillow.'

She wanted *him* on her pillow—and far more dangerous than her want, which was perpetually there, was the clear arrival of his.

Nico's hand came to her cheek and he smoothed a stray lock of hair. It wasn't only Aurora's resolve that was fading.

She floored him.

Always.

The sexual attraction between them was undeniable, for sure. But there was also this banter between them—this life they both knew and this world they had shared. And Nico, despite doing everything he could to avoid it, now did not want the night to end.

His hand remained, cupping her ear, and his fingers were in her hair.

She could remember that hand, pressed over her mouth as she came, and she fought not to kiss it, not to flirt.

She won the former battle but failed on the latter.

'I packed your underwear,' Aurora said in a provocative tone—and there went the express train of her mouth again, saying things it should not and being too familiar.

Not that Nico seemed to mind, for he was stroking her earlobe and his eyes were telling of his desire.

And the guard she had fought to keep up was dissolving, for she did not know how to be anyone other than the person she was. The person who was in love with him.

He brought out the Aurora in her.

'Aurora…' Nico said, and she heard in the sound of him saying her name a summons to bed.

She ached to turn her head just a fraction and kiss the palm that held her cheek, to give in to the bliss of him just one last time. To have Nico make love to her in Rome.

He was leaving in the morning and would return only after she had left. This was their only chance, and Aurora did not know how to resist him.

Her neck fought not to arch and her mouth not to part to kiss his palm.

But then her guardian angels dashed in.

They flew from their clouds, or wherever they'd been hiding, and there was no time for them to apologise for their absence. They hauled her back from the brink.

'Goodnight, Nico.'

Well done, Aurora!

Though it wasn't actually Aurora who had halted things, for she was *desperate* for his kiss. No, it was a force greater than she that had somehow gathered and dragged those words from her mouth.

'It's been a long day,' she added, then gave him a smile and walked off.

It would be a long, lonely night.

But at least she would awake with her pride.

CHAPTER SEVEN

Tuesday:
Room Service breakfast
RSVP'd Marianna to decline Nico's kind invitation to breakfast, explaining I had already made plans.
Social Media Training.
Room Service dinner.
Read for a little while
Cried.

Wednesday:
Breakfast in restaurant.
Forgot about Nico!
Bought a red dress during lunch break.
Worked the day on Reception and was shouted at.
Went to the hotel's hair salon and drank champagne while hair was done!
Read some more.
Hate him.

Thursday:
Woke early
Coffee at sunrise in a café opposite the hotel.
Grateful that I didn't sleep with him again...
Not really...

THERE WAS SOMETHING so special about Rome early in the morning. The gleaming cobbled streets, fresh from the street cleaners, the lack of people, the abundance of all things beautiful.

Everywhere she looked there was more to see.

The disgusting gargoyles with their erections and horrible tongues.

The timeless beauty of the Spanish Steps.

And there it was. The Trevi Fountain, standing resplendent.

Almost alone, Aurora gazed into the water and saw there were just a few coins, so it must have recently been cleaned out. Then she looked up to Triton and his horses and then back down to the water.

All she had to do was throw in a coin to assure her return to Rome.

Never.

Aurora wanted to return to her simple life.

She *almost* meant it.

She would find her fireman, or a man who worked the vines, and she would love him completely, and he would love her in return.

And she would not hanker for Rome.

Nor for sitting in a bar with Nico and the sheer exhilaration of being near him.

And she would not regret that abrupt goodnight. She would be proud of her resolve. For instead of kissing his palm, and going where that would have led, she had called a halt and said goodnight.

Good, Aurora!

And she would say this to her daughter, if God gave her one.

I knew a wicked man once. A man who made my heart both bleed and sing at the same time...a man

*who made me succumb to my wildest urges. A man who
made me believe we had been together in another life,
for even if I did not know him completely I recognised
him in my soul.*

*But I walked away, dear daughter. I did not let him
use me again and again. And I don't regret it. No, not
even for a moment.*

So why was she suddenly crying and scrabbling in
her purse for a coin? Throwing it into the water with
her eyes closed as she wished with all her heart for her
time again…?

Because she would *always* regret Rome and the decision to walk away from the man she would love until
her last breath.

She couldn't tell that to her daughter…

Her wings were unfurling in colours she had never
envisaged, and no matter how hard she tried she could
not stuff them back in.

Aurora tossed in the coin.

*Let me return to you, Nico. Let me in. Make love to
me in Rome.*

She was ashamed of her coin-toss in a way it would
be too complicated to explain to someone else, or even
to herself, but Aurora also felt better for it. And her
mood lifted.

Today she was to work in the Club Lounge, which
the very best of the guests frequented, and she had been
told to dress to impress.

Back in the hotel, her curls fell into perfect shape as
she ran her fingers through them, and she took out the
make-up she had bought and applied it.

A little blusher, but not too much.

Eyeliner. Her new best friend.

Mascara.

And a slick of very subtle lipstick.

Should she wear the red dress, even though Nico would never see her in it?

Aurora couldn't make up her mind.

But first she put on a new bra and panties in the most stunning coral.

They would clash, if she wore the red dress, but who cared? No one was going to see.

Aurora wore the red dress.

She found the Club Lounge rather fascinating.

There was breakfast, and then pastries mid-morning, and even champagne cocktails just before midday for a couple who, Aurora found out, had just got engaged.

'*Complimente!*' Aurora smiled as she placed the drinks down.

She was pleased for them—excited for them as she spied the way they held hands even as they sipped their drinks.

But she was sad for herself.

They knew love.

She looked out at the panoramic view of Rome that the Club Lounge afforded and wondered why all she could think of was Silibri and the temple ruins, and the little house her *nonna* had lived in, and had any-one watered the jasmine? Was Nico there now, strolling around confidently because there was no chance of bumping into her?

'Aurora!'

Realising that she had been daydreaming, and had missed what Marianna had said, Aurora snapped to at-tention. 'I'm sorry. I was miles away.'

Many miles away, in fact—all the way to Silibri.

'I asked if you'd mind going to Nico's. There's some maintenance being done on the balcony. You might be there for a couple of hours. I don't like to ask just any-one, and you *were* there the other day.'

'Of course,' Aurora responded politely, for what else could she say?

'You look nice,' Marianna commented.

'I was worried it was too much for work.'

'Not here, it's not,' Marianna said. 'Every day is like a wedding! Your hair is nice too.'

All her early life Aurora's mother had trimmed her hair, and later Aurora had done it herself. For her confirmation and on special occasions she had gone to an aunt who, until yesterday, Aurora had believed to be a hairdresser.

Oh, no, she wasn't.

Luigi was a hairdresser!

And a therapist.

And an ego-boost.

All rolled into one delicious package.

Aurora had left the hotel salon feeling like a rock star.

Her dark locks felt like silk, and looked as if every strand had been polished by hand. Her hair now fell in a glossy, snaky curtain, several inches shorter than it had been when she had walked through the heavy brass doors.

The cost?

Astronomical.

Almost a week's pay, gobbled up in two luxurious hours.

Actually, *two* weeks' pay had been spent, if she included the dress, but when in Rome…

It was a short trip to Nico's, and the driver gave her his number to call when the maintenance was done.

Soon she would be alone in his stunning villa… But

not quite, for there were two men in overalls who were waiting for her to arrive.

'*Buongiorno!*' Aurora greeted them warmly as she disarmed the security system and let them in. And as she led them up the grand stairs she learned a little more about Nico's home.

It was a heritage building, they said, and the balcony inspection was just routine.

There was nothing routine about Nico, Aurora thought.

His bedroom was exactly as it had been the last time she had seen it, with not a thing out of place.

Except for Aurora!

She was a little unsure of *her* place.

In Silibri, she would have put on coffee for the men, and then gone to chat with them as they worked.

But of course she was not at home, so she hovered in the main bedroom as the men inspected the balcony.

It took mere minutes.

'*Completato,*' the older man said.

'You're finished?'

'*Sì.*'

It really had been a routine check.

Aurora saw them out and then went back upstairs and locked the French doors. She took out her phone to call the driver to come and take her back to the hotel.

Except she didn't make the call.

Instead she stood in his bedroom for what was undoubtedly the last time. The coffered ceiling was a work of art, and she looked at the intricate engravings and wondered if Nico lay on the vast bed pondering how such art had been crafted and by whom.

Or did he lie with the drapes open at night and look out to Rome and Villa Borghese Park? Aurora wondered.

Or was he too busy when he was in bed?

Of all the regrets she had—and there were many where Nico was concerned—her biggest regret was Monday night.

Despite her promise to be aloof and professional, despite her promise to herself to get over him, it was the closest they had ever been.

Two people sharing a drink and conversation.

He had told her he loved his father, and that had been a revelation in itself. And he had been about to kiss her, Aurora was sure.

And take her to bed too.

Her body and her heart had wanted him to, yet foolish pride and her determination to put him behind her had told her no.

She wasn't snooping, Aurora told herself as she wandered around the stunning room. Of course she wasn't.

She was merely checking that everything was in order for Nico's return, just as his PA surely would.

She walked to his bedside and saw the small shelf of books that was beside it. Leafing her way through them, she frowned when she saw they were all books on productivity and increasing focus.

'Nico, how do you relax with this?' she asked out loud.

And then Aurora smiled and reached into her bag— not for her phone, but for the sexy romance she was currently reading. She would slip it into his reading pile, and even if he didn't want *her* she would spice up one of his nights, somehow!

But she hadn't finished reading it herself yet.

Well, she almost had. It wouldn't take her long to do so, and Marianna wasn't expecting her back for a couple of hours...

Putting her bag on the floor, she sat down on the edge of his bed—and, truly, that was how Aurora meant to remain. Except as she read unthinkingly she slipped off her high heels.

Nico would have told her to make herself at home, she told herself as she lifted her legs onto the bed and lay back on plump pillows. Of course he would. Well, if he'd behaved as he should then he would. How many times had he rested his head in her pink bedroom, after all?

It was the most peaceful hour she had found in Rome. There, in his bed.

Now and then she would glance up and look out to the lush green park, and then back to her book she'd go, letting out a contented sigh at the end.

It would be Nico who would read it next!

After she'd leant over and placed the book on his shelf, between his boring other ones, she lay back with a smile, imagining Nico's expression when he found it.

Imagining him.

Imagining *them*.

It was something she knew all too well in her head…

'Aurora!'

It was clearly her day for being caught daydreaming.

His voice startled her and her eyes snapped open. She realised she had dozed off. 'You're back!'

'Clearly.'

In fact Nico wasn't surprised to find her here. Marianna had mentioned that Aurora was at the house, sorting out the maintenance guys.

For the first time in living memory Nico had 'popped home' in the middle of a working day.

And there, in a blood-red dress, with her snaky black curls and bare feet, lay Aurora, asleep on his bed.

He was turned on even before he called her name.

'I wasn't asleep,' she said.

'Then what are you doing?' he asked.

'Daydreaming,' Aurora said, for to her it was the most normal thing in the world to do.

She wasn't flustered. She didn't rush to sit up, and nor did she apologise; instead she looked him right in the eyes.

'About…?' Nico asked, when he knew full well he should be telling her off, or just getting the hell out. For there was seduction in the look she gave him, and he had sustained it with his low reply.

'My husband,' Aurora said. 'My future one.'

'Really?'

'Yes.'

'And what is he like?'

'He has a beard,' Aurora said.

'A beard?'

'*Sì.*' She nodded. 'And when he comes home to surprise me at lunchtime, he laughs when he finds me reading in bed and the house unkempt.'

'Where has he been?' Nico asked, arrogantly assuming she was speaking of him, and of the life they might have lived had he stayed in the village. 'Out working on the vines?'

'No.' Aurora shook her shiny new curls. 'He's a firefighter.'

'I seem to remember you left a firefighter to come home to me,' Nico pointed out, and he could not keep the slight snap of possession from his voice.

'That was for sex, Nico. I'm talking about my *husband.*'

'The one who laughs when he finds you in bed?'

'Not at first,' she said. 'I think he pretends to be cross.'

He stood so still, fighting not to be provoked.

Except a vital part of him was extremely provoked, and he felt her eyes drift there.

'He spanks me,' Aurora said, and with a smirk moved her eyes back up to his.

'That's your fantasy, is it, Aurora?' Nico drawled, trying to sound bored. 'Some bearded man lumbers home and gives you a spanking?'

'Perhaps…' She shrugged. 'What is *your* future wife like?'

'I told you once, but I will tell you again—I will never marry.'

'But if you did, what would she be like?' Aurora persisted. 'Come on, Nico, it's just a game.'

Nico did not and would not play games—not that it perturbed Aurora, for with only her eyes she dragged in the most unwilling participant.

'Tell me about your future wife.'

'She's quiet,' Nico said. 'Undemanding.'

'How nice.'

'I never come home in the middle of the day to find her asleep.'

'She sounds rather boring.'

'I think *demure* would be a better word.'

'No,' Aurora said, and shook her head. 'She bores you so much that I bet you don't even bother coming home in the middle of the day just for sex.'

'Exactly!' Nico said. And it was a most dangerous admission, because it exposed him. With one word he had revealed to Aurora his craving for her. 'I don't come off the phone hard after speaking to her. She gives me no drama, leaves no chaos in my brain. And when I'm working she respects that fact and leaves me alone.'

'Good for her,' Aurora sneered.

She pulled her knees up—not in a deliberately provocative move, more to relieve the ache low in her belly and thighs.

His quick gaze caught a damp patch on her coral silk panties. He didn't know if he had imagined it, but once the idea was in his head he could not rid himself of it.

He should not be playing this game—glimpsing how they might have been. Or rather, he had already played it out in his mind. He should certainly not be sharing that vision with Aurora.

Yet Nico did.

He dragged his eyes from her silk-lined sex and back to her face as he told her some more about his perfect wife.

'There aren't fifty missed calls, demanding to know where I am; there's no, *"Nico, we didn't make love this morning..."*'

He did a lower version of her raspy voice, but it was certainly Aurora that he impersonated, and now they were heading into dangerous territory indeed.

'In fact, when I come home late she doesn't even ask where I've been. She *accepts* that I've been working.'

'She's *so* understanding!' Aurora cooed.

'Yes,' Nico said. 'She is.'

'And do you make slow, boring love to her?'

'There is nothing boring about me in bed, Aurora. But, yes, I make *very* slow love to her.'

She had to remind herself to breathe. 'Does she fake it and let out a little whimper to signal that she's done?'

'No, she *screams* my name.'

Those shaky curls shook as she refuted him. 'I don't think so.'

He crossed the room and decided to lose the stunning view of Rome. He had something infinitely better to look at.

'Not only that,' Nico said. 'She even closes the drapes.'

He did so, and it was unthinkable that he was closing out the busy day he'd had planned.

Not quite unthinkable—because with Aurora he knew this was how life would be. Chaos and tangled limbs. Making up and kisses and heaving tears. Drama from which he had run as a young man as though there was a wolf on his heels.

The heavy drapes blocked out the light, denying him the sight of her body, so he turned on the bedside light and looked down at her.

'Get into bed.'

'But you forgot to switch off your phone, darling,' Aurora said, in the voice of his fabled wife.

Nico wagged a finger to chastise her for the poor imitation. 'She would not ask me to.'

'That is true,' Aurora conceded, for Nico's perfect demure wife would not ask him to do any such thing. And yet she fixed him with a glare. 'But every game has its rules.'

And for the first time—and *only* for Aurora—he turned off his phone, while silently vowing his perfect revenge: she *would* scream out his name.

His eyes roamed her body and made her flood with warmth and shiver at the same time.

'Get undressed and into bed before I turn off the light.'

'Don't turn off the light,' Aurora said, for she wanted to see him.

'But I come home in the *dark*, dear wife.'

She swallowed, and reminded herself of the game they were playing.

It was a little hard to get undressed, sitting on the

bed, and Nico did not help with the zip at the back of her dress. He watched her struggle.

She got the zipper undone and wriggled the dress down instead of up. Took it off by lifting up her bottom and sliding it down her legs.

Aurora could feel that her face was flushed, but not for a second was she embarrassed. Instead she was turned on by his scrutiny, turned on by his silent observation. And wondering how she could even have cared that her underwear might clash when it mattered not.

Again, her hands went behind her back and she unhooked her bra. She heard his ragged breath as, without support, her breasts fell heavy.

Her nipples hurt because they were so erect, and she glanced over and saw his hands that had been clenched by his sides were now undoing his belt.

'Wait,' she choked. 'I want to see you undress too.'

Oh, what was this game they were playing? For they had not so much as kissed, and she was not even in bed—they had not even *started*—but her thighs wanted to squeeze together and her throat was closing with the tension.

She slid down her panties and went to move back the sheets, impatient to get into bed, impatient for his touch. But he growled a word.

'Fermare.'

Stop.

Halt.

Do not cover your body just yet, Nico said with that one word. *Do not remove it from my gaze*.

For on that torrid night, so many years ago, he had not gazed and he had not lingered.

Now he took in the gleaming olive skin and the delicious softness of her stomach, the dark brown nipples that were like searchlights for him and the dark shadow where her shapely thighs met.

He fought not to take her this very second.

He fought not to unzip himself as he parted her legs and take her there and then.

He admired his own control as he removed his jacket.

But it was not quite perfect control, because he could not seem to stop the thrill of anticipation that made his breath shorten.

For it might be daylight on the other side of the curtains, but this was their one night as husband and wife.

And so he dropped his jacket to the floor, and with the same carelessness and impatience discarded his socks and shoes. And then he took off his shirt and felt her eyes reclaim his skin.

Oh, Nico.

She had missed that chest so. It was broad and had a smattering of hair. His long arms were so toned that he *could* have been out working the vines.

Her breath hitched as she watched him remove the last of his clothes.

'You could have had me on Monday night,' Nico said.

'I know.' Her voice was so low and thick that she almost turned around to see who stood behind her, but of course it came from her.

'Why didn't you?' he asked. For that was a side of Aurora that he wanted to know.

'Things were different then,' Aurora said.

Then she had been trying to get over him—then she had been denying the throbbing of her body and the beckoning of his soul to hers and telling herself she did not have to succumb.

But she did not have to tell Nico all that. She did not have to tell him that this very morning she had thrown a coin in the Trevi Fountain and asked to be made love to by Nico in Rome.

She hastily amended that wish.

For now she did not want to be made love to by Nico, she told herself. She wanted powerful sex with him, the way she had known it before.

Aurora was too afraid to know his love and then attempt life without it.

'Please…' she said.

Please come to bed. Please let me know again that flat stomach and those muscular thighs. Let me be taken by you again.

He got into bed.

'Hello, husband,' she said.

And this time when she said it Nico did not roll his eyes.

He turned off the light and lay beside her. 'Are you awake?' he said to the dark.

'I'm awake,' she said, and rolled to face him.

Have me now. Take me now, her eyes told him as they lay facing each other on their sides. *Give me your untamed passion again.*

Instead he spoke. 'Life is peaceful with my wife— calm and without demands.'

Except his heart battered his chest as if he had run home from the hotel and his body was primed.

They faced each other and embraced the war that raged between them.

Her silent screams were for all of him, for Nico's refusal to give anything other than the inches that now nudged her thigh. Aurora wanted his fire and his untamed passion, and she provoked and pushed for the same.

But instead he gave her a taste of slow love.

Just this one time, Nico said to himself. He would give in once and kiss her as he should have on her first time. Not hot, raw sex on a sofa, but deep, slow kisses in his bed.

And while Nico told himself he was giving Aurora the experience she had deserved back then, he was aware enough to know that he wanted it for himself too.

'I should have been more tender then…'

Four years on from *that* night he answered the question she had asked the following morning, and told Aurora his regrets.

'No,' she whispered. 'It was perfect just as it was.'

She was actually scared to know him as tender, but *that* was the kiss he now gave her. A slow kiss that sent her mind dizzy with little arrows of affection delivered by his velvet lips.

His clean, male sent made her ache for more—more of his body, more of his mouth—but she lingered a while in this bliss.

He kissed her slowly. His hand was warm on the back of her head and she almost fought him with her mouth, fought for him to kiss her harder.

Because a taste of his slow love was now a terrifying prospect. The game they had been playing was just a little too much for her heart to recover from.

He removed his mouth from hers.

She did not want him to stop. His mouth, tender like this, made her tremble, and his tongue, his lips caressing hers, demanded her pleasure. She let herself revel in it.

'I should have seduced you,' Nico said.

'You did,' Aurora breathed as she recalled that even with walls between them on that hot, sultry night, desire had coursed through her, just as it was rolling through her now. 'You are.'

He slipped in his tongue and she tasted him again. He devoured her with his mouth and her hands shot to his head, just to feel his hair, just to hold his face so that she never had to separate from this bliss.

Their mouths touched and she found out how powerful his slow kiss could be. For she was not here in his dark bedroom in Rome, and she was not even thinking of that night in Silibri. She was in a place that was reserved on this earth just for them. A place that could be found whenever their mouths met.

He dragged his lips from hers, and then Aurora discovered that there were kisses she still did not know.

He took his hands from her head and turned her with a silent command, so she lay on her back as his mouth met her neck. And the slight suction he made on that sensitive flesh made her gasp.

'Take me, Nico.'

She did not want to linger in this bliss. She did not want to know the tender pleasure of this Nico, for it would surely be safer not to know.

He licked her nipple, making generous wet circles. And she bit on her lip as he blew cool air there. Then moaned as he sucked hard. She felt her hips rise and his hand slip down.

'I want you so badly, Aurora.'

'Take me, then...' she pleaded again.

'I was too rough that night.'

'No, no...' she sobbed. 'You weren't.'

'I should have been gentler for your first time.'

He kissed her stomach. She had always thought it too fat, yet she found she adored her own ripe flesh when it was loved by his mouth.

'I should have tasted you...' He moved down the bed

so that his head was between her legs. 'I should have cooled you with my mouth.'

'Cooled me?' she checked, for she could never have been cooled. And certainly not by what he did now.

'Oh…'

His tongue made deep, slow strokes and he nibbled at places she did not think it right for him to do so, but her hands knotted in his hair and she let him show her bliss.

Nico was turned on by the humming noises she made, but she refused to call out his name. He could feel the tension building in her and the grip of her thighs on his head.

He sucked and he probed with his tongue and though sometimes he licked slowly he did not let up for a second.

He was relentless.

'I—I'm…' she gasped.

He knew.

For how could he not know when her tension was unleashed and she held on to a scream? How could he not know when he was drinking from her pulsing, tender place?

He pulled himself up over her.

Now he would take her—fast. Now this torture would be done. Aurora pleaded with him in her mind, and she knew she should never have made that wish at the Trevi Fountain.

To know his love even just once more would hurt later.

But when he slid into her…when he crushed her with his weight, and when she anticipated his rapid thrusts… she wrapped her legs round him, to join in and bring them both to the delicious end.

And yet his hands removed her legs and now he took

her arms and held them above her head on the pillows as he moved onto his forearms.

'Slow, boring love…' he said.

Aurora heard the creak of the bed and the way his breathing sounded as he strove to hold on to his release.

'Am I boring you Aurora?'

'No…' She no longer knew the rules of the game. For she was burning and melting at the same time.

He released her hands from the trap of his arms. Her fingers pressed into his shoulders and she wanted to dig her nails in, but she did not. Instead, her hands disobeyed her mind and slipped around the sides of his torso, lovingly stroking him, feeling the bliss of his smooth back and sliding her hands over the slight sheen of his skin, exploring the muscles. And then she met his taut buttocks.

Now her head lifted and she offered Nico a devoted kiss.

Better that than sob his name.

Better that then tell him how much she loved him.

She would not give in.

And soon Nico would have no choice but to give in himself, because he was moving faster now, thrusting without any measure of control.

'I want you,' he told her, and he took her faster.

'Nico,' Aurora said, 'I can't do this over and over.'

'You can.'

'I can't pretend I don't want you.'

'Keep wanting me,' he told her.

'I'm scared to keep wanting you,' she admitted.

'*Never* stop wanting me,' he told her.

And those ragged words felt like permission simply to give in.

She collided with the stars, with the darkness, with

the fantasy of husband and wife, with the rush and power of the orgasm *he* had made. She had not known such intensity lived in her and it felt as if she'd been tasered.

'Nico!' She thought she screamed his name, but her throat was so tight it came out as a hoarse cry.

Nico let out his own breathless shout as he drove into her for the final time.

And then they kissed—a breathless panting kiss that sedated her in her post-coital bliss.

He rolled off her and she lay in the dark bedroom, naked and uncovered, for the sheet had long since gone.

And now she found out what he had meant. For she was cooling now. The air on her damp body felt calming, and she could hear his breath evening out as hers did the same.

No, his slow love was not boring.

For even as she lay cooling she knew that at any given moment she would want him again.

Like this.

In his bedroom.

Night after night after night.

Did he regret it already? Aurora pondered as he lay quietly beside her.

Possibly *she* did, for she was replaying his words.

Keep on wanting me.

CHAPTER EIGHT

KEEP ON WANTING ME.

Aurora lay there repeating his words in her head.

Was that to be her destiny?

To keep on wanting him? To keep on being available to him?

That sated feeling was fading, and as Nico reached across her for his phone the doubts and the hopelessness kicked back in.

'Nico, why did you come back to Rome early?'

'Work finished sooner than I expected and I had a good visit with my father, for once.'

Couldn't he just say he had come back so he might see her?

'Can't you give me even the smallest victory, Nico?'

He couldn't.

Instead he sat on the edge of the bed and checked his damned phone.

What was she supposed to do? Get showered and dressed and head back to work?

Sit in her hotel room biting her nails and wondering if Nico would take her out on her last night in Rome?

She was far too easy where Nico was concerned. The sum total of their dating history was having a drink together.

'Nico,' she said. 'Tonight, I would like—'

'Aurora, stop.'

Just stop.

He looked at the endless missed calls and the frantic texts, and knew that if he had been able to choose he really would have preferred to be alone for this moment.

'Pronto?' he said into his phone.

Aurora heard for the first time a slight shake in his strong voice as Nico asked when. And if anyone had been with him. And if his father had been in pain when he passed.

She started to cry.

When he'd ended the call Nico did not speak. Aurora went up on her knees and pressed herself into his back, wrapping her arms around him and crying and kissing his neck. Not in a sensual way. This time she was the tender one. But though she held him, it was Aurora who shed the tears.

Nico did not know how to.

'Your mother took him lunch,' Nico said. 'Then called for the doctor to come quickly. It was peaceful, the doctor said.'

She moved around him so she sat facing him, on his lap, her legs wrapped around his body. She tried to read his face, to measure his pain, but it was blank.

'I shouldn't have come away this week,' Aurora cried. 'I knew he was weak…'

Her tears were genuine, for she had both loved and hated the old bastard. Loved his wit and his humour and his proud ways. Hated that his hands had put bruises on her beautiful Nico, and she detested the insults that had been hurled from his mouth.

'I need to get back,' Nico said.

He prised himself out of her arms, but they sprang back.

'Soon.'

'Now,' Nico said, and stood so she slid off his lap.

He went towards the bathroom and she followed, but he closed the bathroom door in her face.

She stood there with the thick wood between them.

Geo was dead.

Panic thudded in her chest.

She opened the drapes, and although Rome looked the same, as she turned naked from the French windows the bedroom did not. There were rumpled sheets and discarded clothes and the scent of sex in the air.

Aurora saw the chaos she'd brought to him.

He had returned to this.

She dressed. It seemed wrong to be pulling on a red dress when Geo was dead, but she had a black one back at the hotel she could change into.

Aurora wanted to help, and so she thought about what Marianna would do—she would pack, of course, except Nico had not even unpacked.

'What are you doing?' he asked as he came out of the bathroom with a towel around his waist to the sight of Aurora going through his wardrobe.

'Finding a black suit...'

'I can manage.'

'And a black tie...'

'Aurora, go back to work—get on with your job.'

'Work?' She swung around and looked at him aghast. 'How selfish of you! Do you really think we can all carry on working now? We have lost someone too.'

'Cut me some slack, Aurora. I'm not thinking straight.'

He was hanging on by his fingernails even as she turned away in that red dress with tears streaming down her face. It dizzied his mind.

Where the hell was the calm wife from their game? The one who'd pour him a drink and leave him to spend these first moments on earth without his father alone.

Where was the demure woman who would accept his silence and lack of outward grief?

He would like to take Aurora back to bed, right now. To close the drapes and to weep.

'Oh, Nico…'

She was crying again and, frankly, he would have liked to join her.

'Aurora, go back to the hotel. I am going to make some phone calls and then I will be flying back to Silibri.'

'I'll go and pack.' Aurora nodded. Now her phone was ringing. She saw that it was Pino, but did not answer. 'They will all have heard and be wondering what to do.' She looked from her phone to Nico. 'Shall I meet you back at the hotel?'

'Sorry?' He really was not thinking straight. 'Why?'

'Nico, we will be returning to Silibri with you, of course.'

'Aurora, what you guys do is up to you—but I need to get back now.'

'So do we scramble to get a flight and the *cuccette* while you fly in your big plush helicopter alone?'

He sighed, defeated. 'Of course not.'

His driver offered condolences, and in the hotel lobby stood Marianna, looking grim. There too were the Silibri contingent, all dressed in black.

'No one is better prepared for death than a Sicilian,' Aurora commented.

Even in grief she could still make him smile.

'Royalty travel with black outfits too,' Nico pointed out.

'Not always,' Aurora said, and Nico gave a soft laugh.

She disappeared and returned fifteen minutes later, showered and changed, wearing no make up, and he could tell there had been a fresh batch of tears.

Those stunning locks had been washed and her hair was now pulled back in a severe low bun. Her dress was black, as were her shoes, and those gorgeous legs were encased in black stockings.

Yes, these Sicilians were more prepared for death than the Queen of England. And none of them had ever been in a helicopter, which meant there were a lot of shouts and nervous laughter as they took off.

The Silibri contingent had been to Rome but now they were returning.

And they were bringing their Nico home.

CHAPTER NINE

'*CONDOGLIANZE...*'

One by one they took his hand and kissed his cheeks, but all Nico wanted was for this day to be over and then never to have to return to the place that had brought him so much grief.

As the last member of his family, Nico stood alone. There was just this line-up to get through, he told himself. And then his duty would be almost done.

There was to be a small gathering back at the house and then he could return to Rome.

'*Le mie più sentite condoglianze,*' Pino said.

'Thank you for all you did for him,' Nico said.

Aurora was just a couple of people down the line. Soon her hand would find his.

'*Condoglianze,*' Francesca said. 'Nico, he is at peace.'

'I know—thank you.'

Where was his own peace, though? Nico thought, for his head felt like a warzone.

'Nico...' Aurora said.

There was his peace.

A small moment of it in the chaos of a turbulent day.

Her hand took his and he closed his fingers around hers, causing her to look down at their hands rather than up at his face.

'*Condoglianze,*' she said.

'*Grazie,*' he responded, but he did not let her hand go.

She leant forward and kissed his cheek and it was as cool as marble against hers. She kissed the other and then looked at his beautiful mouth, now so pale.

'He thought a lot of you,' Nico told her.

I did it all for you, Nico. I know what Geo did, and I did not respect him for that. But he is...was...your father. Though it was hard at times, I always tried to respect that. I took care of Geo as I would have had you been my husband.

She did not say that, of course. 'I thought a lot of him too,' was her gentle response.

'Thanks for all your help with the arrangements.'

'Of course,' Aurora said.

It was, for Aurora, as simple as that. Of course she would be there for him.

Marianna, who had thought she knew everything there was to know about Nico's life, did not quite know how things were done down here.

Aurora had sat in the house during the vigil, as the villagers came, stayed and went.

That was not the role of a PA.

And Aurora had sat with Nico when he had asked the priest not to speak too much of a Geo having had a loving marriage to Maria, or to go on about his loving son.

'You did love him, though, Nico,' she had said.

And that was not the role of a PA.

But she did not know her own role with Nico. She did not know what part she played in his life. She had been Geo's carer, and at times she had been Nico's lover, but what was she now? His employee?

Still, Aurora had worked hard for this funeral. And she took care of things as a wife would when the mourners moved back to Geo's house. She oversaw the proceedings like a hawk.

The coffee needed to be served more seamlessly, she told Chi-Chi, who was trying to chat up a guy. And the people over there had not been offered food for a while.

Aurora dealt with it all. She was constantly watching, swooping when needed, and then returning to be beside her master.

She looked across the room and could see that Nico was struggling to speak with Pino and his wife Rosa.

'Stay tonight,' Pino said. 'Come and eat with us.'

'Yes, Nico,' Rosa said. 'Don't go back to Rome tonight.'

Aurora, who had been speaking to her father, saw the strain drawing Nico's features taut. She caught his eye and moved to his side.

'We were just saying to Nico he can stay with us tonight,' Rosa explained as Aurora joined the conversation.

'My father has offered the same,' Aurora said. 'But Nico has to get back to Rome.'

'When will you be in Silibri again?' Pino asked him.

'We'll see.'

Aurora felt the cannelloni she had just eaten curdle in her stomach at Nico's vague reply. Nico truly answered to no one.

And then, one by one and two by two, the mourners were gone.

There is no sadder place than a house after a funeral when everyone has gone home, she thought.

Just Nico and Aurora remained. They were alone again. But she was suddenly scared that it was for the very last time. That the next time she saw him it would only be about work.

The cups and glasses and plates were all washed and put away. None of the endless food that had been made and brought was left in the kitchen—Nico had asked his guests to take the leftovers with them.

'You could stay at the hotel if you don't want to stay here,' Aurora suggested as she plumped the cushions in Geo's empty chair and missed the grumpy old man. 'I know it's not open yet, but there are suites…'

'I would rather go home.'

And that made her breath hitch—because *here* was home. Could he not see that?

'When do you think you will be back?' Aurora could not stop herself from asking, hoping that although he had been vague with Pino he might not be with her.

'I don't know,' Nico said.

He had an army of people who would take care of the small paperwork trail Geo had left. And the house…? He would send someone to shut it up properly, and work out what to do with it later.

Right now he wanted to get back to the cool order of his life in Rome.

He turned his mind to answer her question. 'I'll be back for the hotel opening.'

'But that is four months away,' Aurora pointed out, and dread clenched like a fist as she realised Nico was really putting Silibri—and her—behind him.

'Yes.'

'Will you sell the house?'

'Probably.' *Just stop with the questions*, he wanted to tell her, for his head was pounding. 'Yes.'

'But wouldn't it be nice to have a home here? Like you do in Rome?'

'This was never my home, Aurora.'

'I don't mean the house. I mean Silibri…'

'I do too,' Nico said.

He did not have family here. There was no guilt or duty to bring him back to the village. Just work.

And he would soon pass that on. He would get the hotel up and running and then sell it, he decided. Finally he would be done with Silibri.

He would not keep her hanging.

'Aurora, the hotel will be up and running in no time. I will pass on the management of it and then...'

He shared his business decisions with no one, and yet Aurora did not fit into the category of 'no one', so he told her what his grieving mind had decided.

'And then I shall sell it.'

It was too painful for him to be here now. He had done his best for the village, and now his father was gone.

'There is no reason for me to return to Silibri,' Nico said. 'I have not one decent memory of this place.'

Aurora gasped.

Not one? What about that time on the sofa, Nico? Does the night you took my virginity not even rate?

Hawks had talons, and Aurora felt hers then.

She wanted to slap his face, to deliver to him some of the pain he had flung at her. But she was not a violent person. She had never understood how Geo could lay a hand on someone he loved, and she would not lower herself to do it now.

'Not one decent memory?' Aurora checked.

Nico closed his eyes and wished that she had slapped him, for it would have been so much easier to end this on a row. To throw up his arms and feel justified in walking away.

But instead her velvet brown eyes tried to meet his. 'How many more ways can you hurt me, Nico?'

'Aurora…' He already regretted those words. He could both see and hear the hurt they had caused, for her voice was raw and her face was bleached white. 'I should not have said—'

'No,' she interjected. 'Don't bother apologising, or rephrasing, or trying to find another way to say what you really mean. I *finally* get the message, Nico. It's the same one you have been giving me for eight years now. You. Don't. Want. Me.'

If he refuted that, Nico knew that they would end up in bed.

Again.

Or rather they would have sex on the floor, because he could not stand the thought of sex in his father's bed.

Or perhaps they would go to one of the empty suites at the hotel and he would bury himself in her there.

He thought all that even as he stood with her sad vocalisation of his feelings for her ringing in his ears.

And when he did not refute Aurora got her answer from his silence.

Aurora regretted so many things, but somehow— *somehow*—she must not live to regret the moment she left. She must not break down within his sight.

Instead, she was as brave as she could be. 'Live well, Nico,' she said, and kissed his cold, pale cheeks. 'I wish you nothing but good things.'

And finally she let herself out of the house and let Nico out of her life.

CHAPTER TEN

Four months later

'NICO JUST LANDED.'

Aurora, who stood in the cool of Reception, nodded to Francesca. 'Everything is ready.'

The press were here for the official opening of the hotel, and the guests mainly consisted of Nico's wealthy contacts and a few select people from the travel industry, who would be dining in the restaurant and staying in the sumptuous suites on this very exciting day for Silibri.

The real guests would start arriving next week.

Nico had made it clear—via correspondence rather than in person—that he did not want their luxury stay to be encroached upon by the opening celebration.

Nico had stayed well away from Silibri—had not been back since the funeral. And Aurora had never been more nervous in her life to see him—though that had nothing to do with work.

Work was the one thing in her life that was going very well.

The hotel was stunning: each suite had a sumptuous view, either of the ocean or of the ancient temple ruins. Many of the suites had their own private pool, and all had a balustrade balcony made from the same stone as the temple.

It was sheer opulent luxury, and it would change the village economy entirely.

Guests would soon be strolling through the long empty streets. Cafés that had closed and lain empty for years had been renovated and would be opening again—not just for the hotel patrons, but for the fleet of staff who would work at the hotel, as well as their families.

Life was returning to Silibri.

And soon Aurora would have no choice but to leave.

She was pregnant.

In the first few weeks after Nico had left Aurora had been too angry and confused to consider the possibility that she might be pregnant. She had been grieving for Geo, as well as mourning the loss of Nico from her life.

She had buried herself in work and it had been her saviour. She hadn't just worked alongside Vincenzo, but off her own bat had made a gorgeous library of the photos she had taken of the renovations, which now had its own section on the hotel's website.

Her first inkling that something was amiss had come when the new uniforms had arrived. Aurora had at first assumed there had been a mix-up and that she had tried on someone else's.

The jacket had not done up across her generous bust.

The skirt had felt too snug on her hips.

Aurora had checked the label and seen that indeed it *was* her uniform—and then realisation had started to hit.

Stupido!

That had been her first thought as she had frantically tried to remember when her last period had been.

Stupido!

It had been her second thought too—but aimed at both of them. Because Nico hadn't used protection and neither had he asked if she was on the Pill.

And she hadn't told him that she wasn't.

There had been no thought on that balmy afternoon—just his mouth and his hands and his touch and the heaven to which he had taken her.

Aurora had sent the uniform back and today she wore one a full size bigger—already it was too tight.

She could not stand to think of Nico's reaction. He would consider that she had set out to get pregnant deliberately, Aurora was sure. That she was trying to trap him into marriage. It was an old-fashioned village and marriage was still a foregone conclusion for lovers who found themselves in the family way.

Family.

She gave a wry laugh at that.

Nico did not want one.

'Aurora?'

Vincenzo was going through the list of questions that might come their way as they took their separate groups around the hotel. He, of course, had Nico and all the bigwigs, and she had the local dignitaries. It didn't trouble Aurora, for it was an hour that she would not have to spend avoiding Nico's eyes.

'Right, I'm going to the oratory,' Vincenzo said. 'Good luck today. Any questions you can't handle, just refer them to me—though remember I have to leave by eight.'

Vincenzo was appearing on breakfast television tomorrow and could not stop mentioning it.

'Of course I'll remember. You look very smart,' Aurora added, for in his butterscotch suit indeed he did.

'Thank you,' Vincenzo said, smoothing his auburn hair. 'So do you.'

She wore her hair up and had subtle make-up on, but it had taken some considerable effort to conceal her new curves.

Aurora had let out the waistband of her skirt herself, and her breasts were practically strapped down. She was bursting out of everything and was just a day away from telling her family the news—once Nico had safely flown out.

Today, though, he had flown in.

Should she tell him?

It was the question that she both woke and fell asleep to, and then asked herself a thousand times during the hours in between.

And as Nico and his entourage crossed the foyer she asked it again.

Should she tell the man who did not want her—the man who was attempting to cut all ties with her and the village—that she was having his baby?

Or rather, did she tell the man who wanted her only in bed and not by his side that she was pregnant? The same man who had told her as they made love to keep on wanting him.

Oh, she still wanted him—for even from this distance the sight of him jolted her senses and turned her on.

He wore a dark suit, presumably stitched by his usual master tailor, but to Aurora's skilled eye it was looking a touch loose on him.

Nico had lost weight.

Not a lot, but enough that she wanted to race to the chef, scream for pasta and force-feed him. It was the Sicilian way.

But she restrained herself.

In fact, for once, Aurora was a picture of restraint.

'It is good to see you.' She smiled, and shook his hand. And this time, as Nico moved in to kiss her in the way old friends would, it was she who put up her hand to halt him. 'I believe Vincenzo has your people gathered in the oratory.'

'How are you, Aurora?'

'Very well.'

She looked incredible.

Nico knew she had been working frantically, but she looked as if she had spent all these weeks lying on a recliner by the pool in the hot Sicilian sun. The Persian Orange of her uniform was indeed perfect, and brought out the little flecks of gold in her dark eyes. Her lips were plump and shaped in a mild smile.

He tried to gauge her level of hurt, and he checked for hostility in those amazing eyes, but saw none.

For there was none.

She loved him—and that, sadly, was that.

'Aurora,' he said as she went to move off. He spoke with his people and then nodded to Francesca, who took the group through to the oratory. 'I need to see you.'

'Of course.' She fixed on a smile. 'What do you need?'

'Not here,' Nico said. 'Not now.'

Nico truly loathed his treatment of her on the day his father had been laid to rest. He regretted with every fibre of his being the way they had parted.

Her dignity.

His silence.

And he had missed her so. That throaty laugh, that raw passion for everything she did.

How to tell her of the mess in his head?

Where did he begin to explain to Aurora that if he were capable of love absolutely it would be with her?

'Your schedule is very full,' Aurora pointed out.

She did not want to be alone with him; she did not want to fall into his arms, to yearn for his kiss. To sob out that she was pregnant and then witness his dark reaction.

Aurora would tell him from a distance, she decided, then and there, because she felt like putty whenever he was near.

But Nico did not give up.

'Later tonight?' Nico said. 'I shall be done around ten.'

'But I finish at eight,' Aurora said, and tried to inject regret into her voice. 'Perhaps we could schedule a meeting for the morning?'

'I don't want a work meeting.'

No, he wanted sex. Aurora was very sure of that.

Nico was staying in the Temple Suite tonight, and no doubt he did not want to spend the night alone.

Damn you, Nico!

She corrected herself: she was not putty—more, she was a puppet on Nico's string. He thought he could bed her at will. And the real trouble was that he could.

Perhaps she wouldn't even *have* to tell him. She was feeling so hormonal right now that to be alone with Nico meant she would fall into his arms. He would just have to strip off her skirt and he would know. Or his hands would remove her bra and the heavy breasts that were now crushed against her chest would spring full into his hands…

Now he saw anger in her face. It flashed in her eyes and it formed in two red dots on her cheeks. But her smile remained.

'I want to speak to you Aurora,' Nico said.

But it would have to wait, for Vincenzo was making an approach.

'Ah, Signor Caruso!' Vincenzo said. *'Benvenuto!'*

'Welcome?' Nico checked. 'What do you mean, *welcome*? It's *my* damned hotel?'

'What's eating him?' Vincenzo asked as Nico stalked off.

Aurora knew she now had to tell a lie, and she watched Vincenzo's face fall as she spoke. But that lie would keep her sane.

It kept her sane even when Nico joined not the bigwigs' group, but the local dignitaries as Aurora gave them her tour—fully thirty minutes behind Vincenzo's schedule.

First she took them outside to the main pool, where the ruins of a Roman bath had been carefully brought back to life.

'Most of the suites,' Aurora explained, 'have their own private pool, but this is the central one. Though it is positioned so that it can't be viewed from the main building.'

'Why is that?' a reporter asked.

'For private functions,' Aurora said. 'It looks incredible when lit at night, and with the calibre of guests we expect to host we would not want to risk them being photographed.'

'Can a couple book just this area just for themselves?'

'Of course,' Nico answered, when Aurora could not.

She could feel the sun beating on her head, and Nico's eyes on her, and the air felt so thick she could barely drag it in.

Oh, how she wanted to discard the jacket and skirt!

To peel off her clothes and take his hand as he led her into the cool, inviting water.

'Let's head inside,' Aurora said, and deliberately avoided his eyes. 'This was once the oratory, where the monks would gather to pray and meditate,' she explained as they came in from the glittering pool into the huge, cool, dark building. 'The new stone is from the same quarry as the original monastery, and this whole wall…' she touched it lovingly '…is original. Now it's going to be a place for meditation and spa treatments. A place to hide from the world and restore oneself in peace and tranquillity.'

It was truly stunning. All those painstaking hours and millions of euros had been worth it, Nico knew.

Even his father had known. During their last visit, on the last morning of his life, Geo had admitted that he would have sold it to developers.

'But I like what you have done,' he had told Nico. And today Nico held on to those words as Aurora walked them around.

He could *never* palm this hotel off on his managers or sell it.

Yes, he had said that on the day of his father's funeral, and for a while he had thought he would, but as the grief had settled Nico knew he could never just hand it over.

It was his life's work.

'Now…' Aurora smiled as she led them up some stone stairs and across a long cloister. 'I shall take you into my favourite suite.'

'The Honeymoon Suite?' one of the crowd joked.

'No,' Aurora replied.

How could that be her favourite when she would

never know a honeymoon? The truth was she avoided the Honeymoon Suite as best she could.

'This is the Temple Suite,' Aurora told her audience. 'And I'm sure you will soon see why.'

She pushed open the heavy wooden door and as they took one step inside they all gasped—except for Aurora and Nico.

Even the sun had joined the party, and it seemed to split apart the stones of the old temple ruins in this most stunning view. It actually brought tears to Aurora's eyes as she stood and looked out.

'I had seen the temple ruins from every angle I thought possible,' Aurora explained. 'I grew up in Silibri and they were my playground. But some weeks ago I put on a hard hat and was shown the view from here. I admit I cried when I saw the temple from this height and distance. I believe this was the view that the monastery was built to capture. It is a slice of heaven, is it not?'

And it was—except that Nico was watching Aurora, and the way her eyes shone with tears. He could feel her love for this incredible space.

He wished—oh, how he wished—they were here alone.

They would be tonight.

She led them through the suite and onto the huge balcony and was grateful for the gentle breeze to cool her warm cheeks. Yes, she had trained herself not to blush around Nico, but it seemed she could not train herself out of desiring him. The easiest thing in the world, Aurora thought, would be to say yes to Nico.

'Dinner on this balcony would be amazing,' Nico said, as if reading her thoughts.

'Absolutely, it would be,' Aurora agreed.

'I don't think anyone would close the drapes on this.'

Please don't, her heart said in response to his words. *Please don't banter with me and take me back to that day in Rome. Please don't seduce me in this room that I love so much when I know you will only break my heart later...my heart that is trying so hard to mend itself.*

As the crowd moved off, Nico held back and waited for her attention.

'About ten?' he checked.

Aurora swallowed but gave no response.

'You have the key?'

No, she wanted to say, *you have the key. The permanent key. And you turn it, and you open me, and then you close me again. And I cannot be placed on lockdown for even one day more.*

No, she was not yet ready to tell him about the baby.

'I'd better get on,' she told him.

It had been a rewarding though exhausting day.

Aurora had slipped away in the evening, as Nico wined and dined his guests, though he himself barely ate a thing.

Tonight—after this—he would sit on that balcony and he would wine and dine Aurora. And with the temple ruins as their backdrop, he would say what he had come to say.

Nico escaped the celebrations just after ten.

So certain of her love was he that at first it didn't faze him that Aurora was not there.

He ordered champagne and a spritzer. He ordered the freshest pasta, with a light basil and tomato sauce, and for dessert her favourite—Tiramisu. And he asked for the tray to be decorated with wild flowers, picked just before sunset.

All the things he knew she loved.

And he waited.

And then he texted her.

And then he drank the champagne as he called her cell phone but got no answer.

The flowers and the food came, but the meal he had chosen with her in mind went cold beneath the cloches.

Nico put on the television in his room with its most stunning view—just to check the news and be sure that wildfire had not ravaged the village again, nor had there been an accident on the winding roads. For surely Aurora would come if she could…

He woke on the plush sofa to the sound of her laughter and a rare hangover.

The sound of her low, throaty laugh had him looking around the vast suite—and then staring, bemused, at the television.

Aurora looked amazing, with her hair freshly styled, wearing more make-up than usual, and in that gorgeous Persian Orange uniform.

'The Temple Suite,' she said to the interviewer, 'is more than luxury. It is a place where you can retreat, where you can heal, where you can rest and ponder your life choices.'

And it was then that he saw, tucked into the wilting wild flowers, a letter addressed to him. It was clear as he read it that Aurora had intended him to receive it last night.

Nico,
I have told Vincenzo that you want me to do the breakfast television interview. I've lied, but better that than be your plaything again.
*   The concierge can arrange an intimate massage in your suite or, if you do not want Pino*

*knowing your business, you can call Rubina's and
ask Madame to send someone to help you create another unsatisfactory memory of your time
in Silibri.*

    *Sorry to disappoint, but my pride got in the
way.*
Aurora x

And then she laughed again.
At least the Aurora on breakfast television did.

CHAPTER ELEVEN

'*WHAT IS THIS?*'

Back in Rome, Nico wasn't certain he had read things right and was immediately on the phone.

Aurora had resigned.

Aurora Eloise Messina. Now aged twenty-five. With a passion for the hotel like no other and a hunger to succeed, had left.

It made no sense.

He knew full well that she was furious with him. And after the stunt she had pulled Nico had been furious too and had stayed well back.

But his anger was fading now—so much so that whenever he re-read that note he almost smiled.

'Why did she resign?' he asked.

'She was headhunted.'

Vincenzo sounded taken aback that the rather absent owner of the business was immediately on the phone to him the moment the email went out.

'By whom?'

'Aurora would not say. Apparently she was tired of her ideas being dismissed.'

They had *not* been dismissed. Had she turned up for dinner that night then she would have known that.

Nico called her. 'What's all this?'

'Scusi?' Aurora asked.

She was sitting in her little pink bedroom as she awaited a taxi to take her to the station.

Her parents had not taken the news of their daughter's pregnancy well at all—especially as Aurora refused to name the father. A terrible row had ensued.

Nico had been right: her parents *did* snoop, and they had gone through her phone and found the dating app she had downloaded in Rome.

And now she had Nico on the phone.

It was too much for her nerves today.

'Why have you resigned without speaking first with me?' he demanded.

'Nico, I resigned and I have left. I don't have to answer to you when you are no longer my boss.'

'All right, then. Forget that I was once your boss and tell *me*. Why did you resign?'

'So from what standpoint are we talking, Nico? As friends?' Aurora's voice was incredulous and angry, though she struggled to keep the hurt from it. 'Because we are *not* friends, Nico. You yourself told me we could never be.'

'Aurora—'

'Or are we speaking as lovers?' she interrupted. 'But that can't be because you have so many—surely you don't expect them all to give you career updates?'

'Aurora!'

She would not let him in. 'Or are we in a *relationship*, Nico? Oh, but that's right—no. Because you don't want one. You told me—'

'And *you* told me you would never leave Silibri.'

'I was sixteen years old when I said that. Tell me, Nico, is that the only reason you decided not to marry me?'

Silence.

As always, his silence killed her.

She wanted to curl up on her bed and weep into the phone.

Tell him. Tell him about the baby. Tell him that you have never felt so lonely nor so scared.

No!

And Aurora knew why she did not.

'I have to go, Nico. The taxi will come soon.'

It wasn't a lie.

She went downstairs. Her case stood at the front door and her parents sat at the table, looking at the photos the estate agent had taken of her *nonna*'s home.

The home meant for her and Nico.

'The part I don't understand,' Aurora said now, as she stood by the window, still awaiting her taxi, 'is why you would have been happy for me to live there, with a husband who did not love me and did not want me, but you would rather sell that house than give your pregnant daughter a home for her child.'

But they just wanted the problem to go away. By withdrawing their support her parents were assuming that Aurora would be forced to give her baby away.

'Aurora is career-minded,' her mother would declare in the village shop as she chatted to her friends. 'And she's making better money than Nico Caruso paid…'

And then, a few months later, Aurora would return to the village, minus the family shame, and pick up where she'd left off.

That was the unspoken plan in her parents' heads, but deep down they knew Aurora.

She would not be giving her baby away.

'You've bought shame to this family, Aurora,' her mother said. 'How do we hold our heads high when you don't even know who the father is?'

Aurora gave a soft mirthless laugh, for though her mother spoke in anger, it was half true all the same: Aurora *didn't* know who Nico was. Not really.

An ex?

That would mean they had actually been a couple at some point.

A family friend?

Sort of.

Her boss.

Not any more.

'We trusted you to go to Rome,' her mother said, her voice thick with tears. 'We trusted you to behave.'

'It wasn't a school trip, Mamma.'

'Less of your cheek,' Bruno stood. 'While you're under my roof—'

'But I'm *not* under your roof any more,' Aurora said as the taxi finally pulled up outside. 'You've asked me to leave, remember?'

'Because you don't even know the father's name.' Mamma's lips pulled in disgust, as they had when Aurora had first revealed the news that she was expecting a baby.

Tell them. Tell them who the father is. Tell them that you love Nico, your baby's father, with all your heart.

No!

And again Aurora knew why.

There would be shocked gasps, then shouts of anger, but eventually it would be all smiles and delight.

Because Nico would do the right thing by their daughter.

And Nico would.

You could take the man out of Silibri, but you could not take Silibri out of the man.

Oh, Nico might snub some of the village codes, but the basic ones were ingrained.

He would marry her for the sake of their child.

Aurora knew that down to her bones.

Beyond her bones, she felt it in her womb, and she felt it in the place low between her ribs—a little knot that tightened when she imagined their wedding.

Only not the way she had once envisaged it.

Now she saw the villagers' smiles, and heard their cheers, and she could even see the large bouquet she carried to cover her surprise pregnancy—but only for the photos.

Everyone would know about the baby and how delighted the villagers would be. Nico Caruso was putting down roots—back where he had always belonged. And she and Nico would wave and smile and kiss for the cameras, and that night they would lie in bed and have sex because—well, it would be their wedding night.

She could almost feel his resentment as he thrust into her. For Aurora Eloise Caruso had got exactly what Aurora Eloise Messina had always wanted.

Even if Nico never had.

So, no!

She would tell no one the truth.

CHAPTER TWELVE

As the train pulled into Stazione Roma Termini, the main train station in Rome, Aurora felt none of the excitement as she had the last time she'd arrived here.

Then she had been with colleagues, looking forward to training at a luxury Rome hotel. Then she had felt as if her career was on course.

Then she had been looking forward to seeing Nico.

Now...

Aurora did not know.

Yet she had chosen to come to Rome.

Was it in the hope of seeing him?

No, for she dreaded that.

Or had she come with the intention of telling Nico that he was to be a father?

No.

One day she would tell him, but she dreaded that too.

It was more that her world felt safer when Nico was near.

She had arranged accommodation at a very basic hostel, but she would be spending only her nights there. Every day was to be devoted to trying to find work.

But it seemed most restaurants weren't hiring. At least not a visibly pregnant waitress.

And it was the same for cleaning work too.

Every day, on her way to interviews, Aurora passed Nico's grand hotel. And every day, after yet another slew of rejections, she grew more and more tempted simply to land unannounced at his door and demand to see him. To hand over the problem to Nico to deal with.

It was *his* baby after all.

Yet she could not bear the thought of his disappointment, or the way he would reluctantly carry out his duty.

She *would* find accommodation and work and she *would* be in a better position when she told him the truth.

Her family's reaction had hurt Aurora deeply, and if the people who loved her could cast her aside it left her with little hope for Nico's reaction to the news.

But then hope arrived, in the shape of a family of two young children, a stressed mother, and a father who travelled extensively for work. They lived in the Prati district, which was close to Parioli, where Nico resided.

'I need someone for nanny duties and some light cleaning,' Louanna explained. 'Our last nanny left us with no notice...'

'I won't let you down.'

It was a gorgeous old house, and Aurora had her own summerhouse at the bottom of the garden. Louanna was kind, and told her she had all the essentials Aurora's baby would need.

But then she added, 'You will have *three* little ones to care for...'

Aurora knew she would care for ten if it meant she had a home and could provide for her baby. For the first time since she had found out she was pregnant, she felt in control.

But then Louanna's husband returned, and the whole mood in the house changed.

'A pregnant nanny?' he said rudely to his wife. 'What the *hell*…?'

'Shh…' said Louanna as she closed the study door on them. 'Aurora is wonderful and she's a great help to me with Nadia and Antonio.'

As Christmas approached, and Rome grew cold and wet, being in the house was like living in tornado season, Aurora mused. She was watching the news at the moment, holed up in the little summerhouse at the bottom of the beautiful garden, but she kept casting anxious glances towards the house.

Soon the husband would travel again, and peace would prevail, but it was like watching dark clouds gather whenever he came home.

Aurora thought perhaps she had heartburn. Certainly the doctor had suggested that she did, but the burning high in her stomach seemed to coincide with the husband's arrival home and amplified when she saw bruises on Louanna's fragile arms.

'What happened?' Aurora asked.

'I bumped into the door.'

'And the door was shaped like fingers?' Aurora checked, in her usual forthright fashion. 'Louanna, you have to leave him.'

'Where will I go?' Louanna begged. 'Where will *you* go, Aurora? Your baby is due in two weeks.'

'Don't stay for me,' Aurora said.

Yet her heart was twisting in fear at the thought of being out on the streets so close to her due date.

'He is a good man…' Louanna was defensive. 'He just has a lot of stress at work.'

Nico had a lot of stress at work, Aurora thought, and he would never have carried on like that. She had never hidden her smile or her sass from him.

Call Nico, her mind said.

But then she caught sight of her reflection, her ripe body and troubled eyes, and she knew she did not want to land on him like this.

Not like this.

But soon the tornado had left again, and with the husband away on business the last few days of her pregnancy were among the nicest she had known.

She went to church with Louanna and the children, to watch the nativity play that Nadia was in, and it brought tears to Aurora's eyes. Louanna took the kindest care of her, and Aurora felt so spoiled when she woke to breakfast in bed one morning.

But the storm clouds were gathering again, for tomorrow Louanna's husband would be home.

That night Louanna made the supper. The children were sweet, and seemed to understand that Aurora was tired, and asked over and over again about her baby.

'I hope it's a girl,' Nadia said as Aurora lay on the sofa, scrolling through baby names on Louanna's laptop.

'I hope it's a boy,' said Antonio.

'What do *you* want, Aurora?' Louanna asked.

'I want this baby out of me,' she admitted. 'I'll take what comes, but I am ready for my baby to be born.'

'Have you chosen a name yet?'

'No,' Aurora admitted. 'I still have no clue. Maybe Nico…' She wasn't going to call her baby that, but it was such a relief to say his name out loud. 'Nicole, if it's a girl, but I love the name Nico.'

Nico.

Nico.

Nico.

She would say it at the end of every breath if she could.

Oh, when would these feelings end? she asked of herself, and foolishly looked him up on the computer.

Nico's world had clearly carried on very nicely without her. The woman with him just last month was blonde and pretty and petite. Then there was a beautiful red-head, who seemed to be getting him through the Christmas festivities.

Nico.

Louanna put the children to bed, and when she came down she gave Aurora a gentle talking-to.

'Do you know who the father is?'

She had asked before and Aurora had been evasive.

'Yes.' She was too tired to lie, but she would not name him. 'And I believe he would support me and would insist that we marry.' She looked over to Louanna. 'But I would rather be alone than live in an unhappy marriage.'

Louanna started to cry.

They spoke for a long while, and then Aurora headed down to her little summerhouse.

Deep in the night she lay restless and unable to sleep. She tossed and turned, and then got up and paced when it dawned on her that the ache in her back was not perhaps just from being heavily pregnant.

Aurora headed into the main house and made a drink. She looked out at the cold, pink morning sky and admitted to herself the very real reason she had not contacted Nico.

He might marry her, but he would never love her.

She would be his Silibri wife.

His mountain wife.

Living in the hills and tucked away.

Made love to when he returned to survey his grand hotel and then put on hold when he returned to Rome.

Or Florence.

Or England or France.

She wasn't sophisticated enough to hold his arm and smile serenely as he conversed. Neither was she calm enough to stand holding the baby and wave him off with a smile. Nor was she discreet enough to turn a blind eye to his philandering ways.

And there *would* be philandering ways, Aurora was quite sure of that.

She had no experience, save for Nico. No tricks to keep him amused. Just her.

And being almost nine months pregnant, and already rejected as his bride, wasn't a brilliant combination to inspire confidence.

Aurora would not be able to stand being a small part of his life—to live in the background. She was pure Sicilian and lava ran in her veins. She burnt at the thought of Nico with someone else—and, no, she would *not* stand back in dignified silence.

She moaned in horror at the thought of it.

'Aurora?' Louanna stood at the kitchen door. 'Are you okay?'

'No…'

She was scared and she was pregnant and she loved Nico so much that it hurt.

It hurt.

'I can't do this,' she admitted.

'You *are* doing this, Aurora,' Louanna said. 'Your baby is on its way.'

Aurora had changed her mind. 'I'm not ready.'

But the baby was.

She was in labour—without the man she had loved all her life by her side.

That was the hard truth, wrung from her soul as she bore down and gritted her teeth and knew she would rather be alone that accept his crumbs.

No matter if those crumbs might be solid gold and would provide for her baby and keep her in style.

'I hate him!' she shouted as she gripped her thighs in the delivery suite and bore down.

'Stop shouting and push,' the doctor said.

But Aurora ignored medical advice and carried on with her rant. 'He wants his freedom—he can have it!' she declared loudly. 'I'll survive better without him.'

Aurora did not pick up on the midwife's smile, but she got her support.

'Yes, you will! Come on, Aurora—use that anger to push!'

She was furious, and it felt so good to be angry as she pushed her baby out. 'I've *got* this,' she declared.

'You have, Aurora,' the midwife said. 'Come on—another big push.'

She was raging, and fury gave her strength, and she pushed with all her might…

And then fury left as love came rushing in—the purest love as she glimpsed her son.

He was long, and he had a lot of thick black hair, and huge navy eyes, and a dent in his chin as if an angel had stamped it there. His huge mouth let out husky and indignant cries.

She reached out for him with a love so fierce it pierced her soul. For the baby was the perfect blend of her and Nico. She laughed as she kissed him, for after one look not a person in her family or in the village would need to ask who his father was.

'He's beautiful!' she cried. 'He's perfect. My baby!'

Her baby—and also a real tiny person, who cried and seemed soothed when she held him. His eyes seemed to recognise her, for he held her gaze and fell quiet.

She had never fathomed that love for her son would be so immediate and so intense.

He was worth all the pain and fear and Aurora knew she could take care of him.

Louanna and the children came to visit her on the ward.

'Oh, Aurora…' Louanna said as she held the tiny little boy. 'He is perfection. Have you thought of a name?'

'Gabriel,' Aurora said. 'God-given strength.'

'Have you told your family?'

'Not yet.' They could wait.

'What about—?'

'I just want to get used to being a mother,' Aurora cut in. 'I want some time with my baby and to know what I'm doing. I want my confidence back.'

And Gabriel brought extra blessings! A little postpartum haemorrhage on the day Aurora was due to go home meant a trip to the operating theatre and staying in hospital for a few extra days.

Which meant that Christmas was over and Louanna's husband had gone by the time she brought her baby home.

It was a golden time.

The first two weeks passed by in a blur and she lived on Gabe's schedule.

He was such a sweet, quiet baby, and even when the husband came home Aurora did not notice as she was holed up in the summerhouse, getting to know her tiny baby.

When snow filled the garden and painted everything white, he went to South Africa for a couple of months.

Louanna was happy.

Aurora could not believe her luck to have found this gorgeous family that was allowing her to provide a home for her baby.

When Gabe—as he had become known—was eight weeks old, she walked little Nadia to school in the slushy snow, pushing the pram as Antonio skipped by its side, and then waving off the little girl.

'Today,' she said to Antonio as they walked home, 'we will make lasagne.'

'Can I roll the pasta?'

'You can,' Aurora said. 'But you have to roll it thin and not get bored like last time.'

Cooking always helped Aurora to think. And soon Gabe was asleep in his little bassinette and Antonio was helping to mix the dough.

She felt as if a fog was lifting. Not that she had returned to her old self, because along with Gabe a new Aurora had been born.

And on her next day off she would call Nico!

It came to her like a flash, and was followed by another rapid thought.

No, she would call Nico tomorrow. And if he wanted to meet her she would be free the next day to meet him—*with* Gabe.

She would not be asking Louanna to watch her son. Nico could get used to the idea, just as *she* had had to.

'You look happy,' Louanna commented.

'I am,' Aurora said, and then looked up to see her employer's pinched face. 'Are *you* okay?'

'Of course I am.' Louanna smiled. 'My husband just called—he's coming home a few days early.'

'Oh, when?' Aurora's voice was as strained as Louanna's smile.

'Tonight.'

'Then it's just as well I've made plenty to eat,' Aurora said.

He came through the door all smiles, and Aurora decided she must have imagined his dark moods, for he was pleasant to everyone.

Perhaps pregnancy had made her tired and more sensitive, Aurora thought as she put little Nadia and Antonio to bed and then came downstairs, to where Louanna was serving up the lasagne that Aurora had prepared.

'Eat with us,' he insisted.

'No, really.' Aurora smiled. 'I'm going to take my supper down to the summerhouse and settle Gabe. Have a nice evening.'

She wasn't avoiding him. The truth was that Aurora wanted to work out what she would say when she spoke to Nico.

'Nico,' she practised aloud, 'there's something I have not told you...' Or, 'Nico, this will come as a surprise...'

She fell asleep, still undecided how to break it to him, and woke to Gabe's cries at two a.m.

'Hey...' she said as she gave him his bottle.

Aurora loved these middle-of-the-night feeds—the contented noises her baby made; the way his fat little hands held hers as she fed him. There was no time more precious to be holding her son as when the world was so peaceful and quiet.

Except tonight the world was not so peaceful and quiet—there was a light on in the main house. Louanna and her husband must be up.

Aurora's heartburn returned as she lowered little Gabe into his bassinette and he slipped back to sleep.

She should just go to bed, Aurora told herself. It was no business of hers.

But as she listened Aurora changed her mind, and wondered if she should call the police.

Which would have been the sensible choice.

Except Aurora was bolshie and passionate, and she did not know how to look away…

CHAPTER THIRTEEN

Rome

THE GLORIOUS SIGHT of the city at night, from the vantage point of his helicopter, did not lift Nico's spirits and there was no sense of relief to be home.

With wealth, Nico decided, came too much cream.

Here in Rome the chefs had been drilled as to his preference for plain food, but it hadn't translated so well at the Silibri site. There the chefs had seemed determined to impress, but they had failed. Oh, the food had been spectacular, but for the first time Nico had heartburn.

Or was it more a sense of unease as he disembarked from his helicopter and saw his regular driver waiting for him?

'I thought you were on leave?' Nico said.

His driver and his housekeeper were married, and Nico had expected a stand-in driver to greet him.

'My leave starts tomorrow,'

Nico glanced at the time. 'It already *is* tomorrow.'

'Perhaps, but better a familiar face to greet you than a stranger. How was the trip?' his driver asked.

'Fine,' Nico responded. 'It went well.'

By all accounts it had been amazing. The new hotel

was sumptuous, and naturally he had his choice of suite there, so when he visited Silibri there would be no awkward stays with neighbours. He had visited the cemetery and knew his father was finally at peace. The hotel was thriving, with the rich and famous and even royalty reserving their spaces. It was wonderful to see the village come alive again.

Yet there was no Aurora.

And without her, without even the slightest chance of bumping into her, Silibri had felt more than ever like a ghost town.

He wished his driver all the best for his vacation and then let himself into his immaculate house. He left his case in the hall and went straight upstairs.

He stripped and showered. Got into bed. Though tired, he was restless. It was months since he and Aurora had last spoken, yet their last meeting still replayed in his head as if it were yesterday.

Why the hell couldn't he move on?

Aurora had. As he had wanted her to do for so long.

He needed distraction, so he climbed out of bed to select a book. He was more than aware that he had lost focus of late.

And then he frowned when he saw a book he didn't recognise on the shelf by his bed.

He laughed as he flicked through it—but then the laugh caught in his throat, because he had never shared his laughter with her.

Not really…

He turned off the light and lay there, thinking of a home that was far away, and the home he now lay in, and the world he had made for himself in Rome.

His driver had been right.

Better a familiar face to greet you than a stranger.

Aurora had always been the familiar face when he went to Silibri. Aurora had been the one he had tried to avoid yet nevertheless had found himself seeking out, and she had *always* made things better.

But now when he went to Silibri it was as if she had been erased.

Bruno hardly mentioned her, and her mother spoke only about Aurora's fancy new career that rendered her too busy to come back just yet. 'Maybe soon...'

And then Nico's eyes opened in the dark.

Hadn't he heard those same frustrating words growing up? Known the code of silence when Pino's daughter had suddenly left school and gone to take care of her aunt in Palermo.

She had returned a few months later, pale and gaunt and with the saddest eyes.

But not Aurora, surely?

Nico sat up.

She would tell him if she was pregnant.

Wouldn't she?

He went over and over that last conversation and within it he found not a clue.

Over and over he replayed it.

Not one clue.

Until the very end.

'The taxi will be here soon.'

Bruno had a car. Why would he not take his daughter to the station on the day she left home?

There was only one reason Nico could see.

His heart was jumping in his chest and he wanted to reach for his phone and call her. But it was the middle of the night. And anyway, she might not answer. Or even if she did she might not reveal anything.

Tomorrow.

Tomorrow he would have Marianna find out just where Aurora had relocated to and then he would call her.

He just had to get through this night.

Rome was not so beautiful this early morning. It was still dark, and also it was freezing cold. She only had with her a few hastily grabbed necessities for Gabe.

But she had her baby, Aurora told herself, and he was unharmed and safe and she cradled him close.

What to do?

She had always wondered why Nico had chosen to sleep in a park rather than in her family home, and now she knew—pride.

But she had a son.

Their son.

And Gabe deserved better than to be outside on a freezing cold morning.

She had never wanted to call Nico like this. She had wanted to be calm and together when she told him. But that choice had been taken from her now.

What if his number had changed or he had blocked her? Or what if he had taken her advice and started turning off his phone at night?

For once she was grateful that he had not.

'Aurora?'

Something inside her jolted. Her name must be on the phone he carried with him. He knew it was her.

'Nico, I am sorry to call—'

'*Never* be sorry for calling me.'

He sounded so calm and so steady and so *nice* compared to the hell she had just left.

'Where are you?' he asked.

'Sitting on a bench in the Prati district.' She gave him the specifics.

'I am ten minutes away,' Nico said, for the streets would be empty.

Make that eight minutes, because he dressed so hastily and continued speaking to her as he climbed in his car. 'What's happened?'

'I don't want to talk about it.'

'Okay.'

Sometimes she was grateful for the sparseness of his words, and grateful too that he did not fill every silence.

Aurora took a deep breath. 'Nico, there is something I have to tell you before you get here. It's not just me. I have my baby with me...'

'Okay.'

No questions.

Not even one.

And then she saw an expensive black car slow down and come to a stop. She found she could not bear to see the disappointment in his face, so as he got out and came towards her she looked down at Gabe.

'He's here,' she told her son.

'Aurora.'

She looked up, and standing there, in a heavy black coat and with snow in his hair, was Nico.

And Rome, early in the morning, was suddenly beautiful again.

'You haven't shaved.'

'Would you have preferred to sit a while longer on that freezing bench while I did?'

'No,' she admitted, and was surprised that he smiled.

She opened her mouth to speak again, but did not know what to say.

Nico spoke first. 'Not here,' he said. 'Not now.'

Instead, he took off his coat and wrapped it around both her and little Gabe and led them to the car.

'My car is just here—let's get you both inside.'

Both.

He said it so easily, but the word felt as if it pierced his brain, for there were two of them now.

Nico didn't quite know what he meant by that, but as he drove back to his home it played over and over…

There were two of them now.

The gates opened on their approach, as they had the first time she'd arrived. How had she ever thought his home intimidating? Aurora wondered as she stepped inside. It felt so delicious that she closed her eyes for a moment and breathed in the scent of Nico's home.

'What do you need for…?' He hesitated. 'Is it a boy or a girl?'

'A boy,' Aurora said. 'Gabe.' She swallowed. 'Well, he's Gabriel, but he's become Gabe.'

'What does Gabe need?'

'Everything,' Aurora said, her eyes filling with tears. 'I just have this bag…' It was enough to get him through the next six hours at best.

'I will call Marianna,' Nico said, and Aurora guessed that was often his solution to irksome things. 'What happened, Aurora?'

'I already told you,' she said, taking a seat on one of his plump couches. But instead of sinking into it she perched on the edge. 'I don't want to discuss it.'

'Perhaps…but you have a bruise on your cheek.'

'He didn't mean to do that.'

She looked up and saw Nico's face stretched into a grim smile.

She *knew* that look.

For she had seen it the night they had first made love. She had seen it when he had lifted her hips from his body and told her to go to bed, and she had said no.

It was the look he gave as his patience slipped away. It was the look he gave just before that steely control dissolved.

'Okay,' she said hurriedly. 'I'll tell you.'

And so she told him—about the job she had taken, and how wonderful Louanna and the children had been.

And then she watched his jaw quilt in tension when she told Nico about the husband.

'Things were fine when he was not there, but then...' Aurora said. 'I was desperate, Nico, and so I stayed.'

She saw that black smile which was not really a smile return to his face. Whatever she had said had clearly displeased him, so she moved on swiftly.

'This morning, at about two, I was putting Gabe back in his crib after feeding. I live in the summerhouse...'

'In winter?'

'It's heated. I was so happy there. Anyway, I saw a light, I saw them fighting—or rather I saw him hit her—and I...' She swallowed. 'I intervened.'

Silence from Nico.

'I couldn't just do nothing.'

'So you ran across the garden—I assume it is snowing there too—and stepped into a house where there was a raging man... Did he hit you?'

'No—no! I was trying to get him off his wife and he pushed me, and then he told me I was not welcome in his home and that I'd caused too many problems with his wife. Then he pushed me again and I fell.' She shook her head. 'I don't want to talk about it any more.'

'Fair enough,' Nico said. 'It will be exhausting enough going over things again with the *polizia*.'

'I'm not speaking to the *polizia*,' Aurora said urgently.

'So you want me to go round there and kill him?'

'Nico, it's a bruise.'

'Get it photographed while it's visible, and tell the police the details while they're fresh in your mind. Or,' Nico repeated, 'I will go round there now and I kill him.'

'Oh, grow up!' she sneered. 'What's that going to solve?'

'Plenty for me.' Nico shrugged. 'So what's it to be?'

'Nico, I don't want to cause trouble. I just want to forget—'

'You will *never* forget,' Nico interrupted. 'And nor will Louanna and the children,' he added. 'I know that for a fact. Ignoring and denying and sweeping things under the carpet does not improve the situation one iota. It needs to be faced.'

'Leave it, Nico, please.'

He did not.

Sometimes she forgot that Nico was just as Sicilian as her.

Nico's stunning apartment became busy with two uniformed police officers, who took a detailed statement. It was exhausting, but there was relief at the end, when Aurora asked if Louanna would be safe.

Nico answered for the police. 'She will be fine. Right now she is tucked up at my hotel with the children.'

When the police had gone, Aurora turned to him. 'You didn't have to do that.'

'It was my pleasure,' Nico said. 'I will ensure she is looked after and I will have my lawyers help her.' He saw her bemused frown. 'Louanna gave you a home when you needed one, and—' He stopped whatever he had been about to say. 'Go to bed,' he told her.

'I can't. Gabe is asleep,' she said. 'I don't like to bring him into bed with me in case I smother him.'

Yet she was tired—terribly so. All the adrenaline that had fired her seemed to have left en masse.

'I could maybe take a drawer and put him in it. Or if you have a box…'

'Or I could hold him.'

It was Aurora who was silent now.

'Surely that's better than a box?' Nico said.

'I sleep better when he is next to me.'

'Let me hold him, Aurora.'

She handed Gabe to him and he took the baby awkwardly and held him in one arm.

'You have to support his head.'

'I am.'

'And if he wakes there are two bottles left. I should put them in the fridge…'

'Go to bed, Aurora.'

'Which bed?'

She flushed as she asked the question—and then Nico took her breath away.

'The one he was made in.'

Such a direct answer—and it told her that Nico did not doubt for a second that the baby was his.

It was actually a relief to close the bedroom door and be alone.

Nico knows.

How he felt about being a father was another matter entirely, but she felt a sagging of relief that he finally knew.

The bed was unmade, Aurora saw. Of course it was—he would have been asleep when she called.

Her book was on the floor beside the bed, and it made her smile that he must have read it—or at least found it.

The shower was bliss—and so, too, was it bliss to put on not a crisp clean shirt, but the one he must have taken off last night that smelled of him.

She slipped between sheets that held his cologne and the male scent of him—and then the door opened and he stood there, holding a cup in one hand and their son in the other.

'Sweet milk,' he said. 'Do you want something to eat?'

'No, milk is fine.'

'I've called Marianna. She is getting some essentials and will sort out a nanny.'

'I don't need a nanny.'

'Well, *I* do,' Nico said.

'Ah, yes, you have a very busy social life.' She fixed him with her eyes. 'What with balls and trips to the theatre...'

'That was in the run-up to Christmas,' Nico said, though he knew full well what Aurora was getting at. Those had been high-profile functions he had attended, and there were photos everywhere. 'It has been a busy couple of months.'

'I saw,' Aurora said, and attempted to slice him in two with her eyes.

Nico held her gaze. He did not blink and then he spoke. 'One thing, Aurora...' He just could not let go of what she had said for a single moment longer. 'You were *never* desperate.'

'So had I arrived here eight months pregnant, with fat ankles—?'

'You know the answer,' he interrupted. 'You were *never* desperate.'

No, because she had the golden ticket—his baby. And, whether he wanted her or not, Nico would see to his duty—and she would have done anything to avoid that.

'Yes, Nico, I was.'

He closed the bedroom door and headed through to the lounge. He looked into navy blue eyes, and saw the groove in Gabe's chin that mirrored his, and then went back to gazing into those sumptuous eyes.

'Your mother,' Nico said to his son, 'is the most difficult woman on the face of this earth.'

And then he fell in love—because an eight-week-old could win a heart with a smile.

'You did *not* inherit that smile from me,' Nico said.

He had both of them now.

Two hearts that he had to take care of.

Two lives that twined and twisted into his.

When he had never even wanted one.

Aurora slept for a couple of hours and then woke to the sight of a crib by the bed.

And the weight of Nico's arm over her.

He was on top of the bed, not in it, and he was asleep.

She wriggled out from under his arm and sat up on the edge of the bed. She peered into the crib at her son, and for that moment all was right in her world.

'He wanted you,' Nico said sleepily. 'I couldn't get him to settle in the crib, but the moment I carried it in here he fell asleep.'

'I didn't hear you come in.'

'You were out of it. Come back to bed. Sleep when he does.'

'No, I'm awake now,' Aurora said. 'And I'm hungry.'

But the deeper truth was she was nervous beside Nico. Nervous of the conversation to come and not sure how she was going to react to his weary, inevitable proposal.

There would be questions first, and accusations, but something told her that a proposal of marriage would come at the end of them.

Happy now? his eyes would say.

No—for she had never wanted to force him into doing his duty like this.

'I'm going to make something to eat...' Aurora said.

'There's a meal being delivered in an hour.'

'A meal being delivered...?' She frowned.

'I often have the hotel chefs prepare my dinner.'

'Well, I just want some bread,' Aurora said. 'Do you have that in your fancy house?'

'I'm not sure,' he admitted. 'I don't do the shopping. Marianna brought a lot of stuff over for Gabe...'

'What did you tell her?'

'Nothing,' Nico said. 'I just told her to arrange a nanny and that I needed stuff for an eight-week-old baby.'

'And she didn't ask any questions?' Aurora looked over at him, and felt a delicious teasing in his vague answers.

'She asked if you were breastfeeding.'

'What did you say?'

'I said that I believed not.'

'I wasn't able to,' she said.

'Well, there's plenty of formula and bottles, and there's an emergency nanny on her way. There is a separate wing in the house, and she shall have Gabe with her at night.'

'No.'

'Aurora, even aside from the bruise, you look terrible.'

'Thank you for being so tender in your assessment of me.'

'You are exhausted.'

She was… Not from the birth—the fog had lifted from that. And not from the night feeds, nor the drama of Louanna and her husband.

It was from eight years of chasing his love and running from his love and then chasing it again.

'You look tired too,' she observed.

'Because you're exhausting, Aurora,' he said, and then he smiled.

The nanny arrived a little while later, and as Nico went to the entrance hall to let her in Aurora sat there, feeling on the back foot, still dressed in his shirt because her clothes were being washed. She braced herself for someone brisk and efficient, as all the people Nico hired in Rome seemed to be.

Instead she was a… Well, all Aurora could think of was a vast Italian *nonna*, who hugged Aurora as if she had raised her and was besotted as soon as she saw Gabe.

'He looks just like his daddy!'

'That's the assumption we're working on,' Nico said, to the nanny's bemusement, but it made Aurora laugh.

And as the nanny got to know Gabe, so he wouldn't get a fright when he woke in the night and saw her, Aurora and Nico ate dinner. A gorgeous *osso bucco* in a wine and herb sauce. There was even bread! Well, there were rolls…

And as they sat at his gleaming dining table, and dinner was served by staff from the hotel, Aurora's stomach growled as wine was poured.

Nico must have sensed her discomfort and dismissed the staff back to the hotel. *'Grazie,'* he said.

'But dessert…' one of the waiters said.

'We can manage.'

Manage.

That was what he would do, Aurora thought. Nico would manage this situation as best he could.

'I'm sorry to have landed on you,' Aurora said.

'I'm glad you called.'

'Please, Nico, don't be polite.'

'Okay,' he said. 'I won't be polite. Are you wearing underwear?'

She gave a shocked laugh, but then her smile faded as she felt his eyes on her.

And then Nico was serious. 'I *am* glad that you called.'

'Truly?'

'Yes. I just wish that it had been sooner.'

'And what would you have done?'

'I'd have done better than a summerhouse in winter.'

'Please don't…' She was starting to cry. 'I did my best, Nico. I got us into this…' She looked at him. 'You think I trapped you.'

'Did I say that?'

'Nico, I wasn't on the Pill.'

'And I didn't use a condom.'

'But you *thought* I was on the Pill.'

'Aurora, I am arrogant, yes, but not arrogant enough to expect you to remain on contraception for me because of one night four years ago.'

Oh.

'If you had actually told me that day that you were

ovulating I don't think I'd have even heard. I was going to have you—'

'Oh!' She said it out loud this time.

Actually, she was surprised he knew such a word—but then the witch in her head flew in and reminded her that Nico knew *all* about female anatomy.

'We made love and we made a baby,' Nico said.

'Yes.'

'I came back from Silibri early because it stunk without you,' he told her. 'Thank goodness I had that last morning with my father, but I flew home early. Marianna said you were at the house, for the balcony...' He looked right at her. 'I came in and I knew you were still there. I followed my desire up the stairs and we seduced each other—the way we do and the way we always have. We took each other beyond the edge and, no, I was *not* thinking of pills, or condoms, or anything other than getting inside you. So, no, you did not trap me.'

'Thank you,' she said.

'And another thing,' Nico said. 'My intention is not to lay a finger on you until we have talked this out, however, please go on the Pill—because there will be times, like this current one, where I want you on the floor.'

'I am on the Pill,' Aurora said.

Thank goodness, she thought, because she was squirming with how turned on she was.

'Why?'

'Because whatever our feelings are, or are not, we do always seem to end up in bed.'

'We do,' Nico agreed, and took a long drink of red wine. He held it for a moment in his mouth, then swallowed it down. 'But not now, because we have a lot to sort out.'

'I'm not ready to sort it all out.'

Tears were filling her eyes again. She did not want his practical solutions, she wanted his adoration—his relief that she was back in his life. Aurora wanted his love.

'Please, Nico, I'm not ready to thrash things out with you.'

'Then eat.'

She nodded.

'But I mean it, Aurora. No sex till we're sorted.'

'Good!'

She took a mouthful of her own wine and swallowed that lie.

For the first time in her life Aurora left dirty plates at the table. She was simply too drained and exhausted as she searched out the nanny. Her room was miles away!

'He's a delight,' the nanny said as Aurora took over bathing Gabe. 'Why don't I warm him a bottle?'

'Thank you,' Aurora said.

It was nice to sit in a chair and feed him, with this kindly woman watching on. She had missed her *mamma* so much these last few months.

'I hope you're settled in okay?' Aurora said.

'And you.' The nanny smiled. 'And little Gabe. It's our first night here for all of us.'

'True.' Aurora gave a tired laugh.

'Your cheek…?'

'It wasn't Nico,' Aurora said, in an effort to clear the air. 'He would never, ever do something like that.'

'I know,' the nanny agreed. 'Or I would not have taken the job.'

'I worked for someone who did, though,' Aurora said.

Oh, heavens, she was like a leaky tap all of a sudden,

but it dawned on her how much tension she had lived with these past months. All the energy spent watching the gathering storms.

Poor Louanna, Aurora thought. And Antonio and little Nadia.

She looked down at Gabe, whose eyes were heavy and sleepy. He gave her a soft smile, at the very edge of his lips and looked at her with his trusting eyes.

Poor Nico.

It hit her then, fully, just how appalling it must be to be beaten by someone you love—someone you should be able to trust.

It was no wonder Nico did not want anything more to do with love.

'Go to bed,' the nanny said when she saw Aurora's tears. 'I'll take care of little Gabe.'

Nico and the nanny were right, Aurora thought as she kissed her son goodnight. She needed a night to sleep properly, knowing her baby was safe.

There was a surprise in the bedroom.

And not just that Nico had straightened up the bed. He stood there in his black lounge pants.

Aurora laughed. 'I thought they were in case you had to go to hospital.'

'Marianna talks too much,' Nico said. 'But, yes, these are for emergencies—and you, Aurora, are always that.'

She did not know quite what he meant, but he'd said it almost fondly.

Nico knew what he meant. She brought drama and tension into Nico's life every time he saw her. She made the blood race through his veins and sent warnings screaming into his brain.

And always he fought to keep a cool head and control. The one time he hadn't, or rather the few times he hadn't...

But he must not think of sex now—he just did not want Aurora out of his sight.

At first they lay in a silence that was neither easy nor companionable; it was just silence as they both burrowed deeply into their own thoughts.

It was Aurora who broke it. 'I don't like leaving Gabe's night feeds to the nanny.'

'Well, try not to disturb me when you get up to go to him.'

She laughed in the darkness, and it scared her how right it felt to be in his bed.

'Did it hurt?' Nico asked. 'The birth?'

'Agony!' Aurora said.

'You didn't tell your parents I was the father?'

'No.'

'Why not?'

'I don't want to answer that, Nico.'

'Okay.'

'I don't want to talk any more.'

'Then don't.'

Aurora liked it that he did not push her to respond, and that he'd accepted her refusal to answer. She liked the feeling of being next to him in the darkness, even if he might not really want her there.

And so they slept—albeit restlessly.

Aurora rolled into him and rested her head on his chest, and then she found her fingers wanting to explore the dips in his ribs, and the hair on his stomach, but before she caved in and did, Aurora rolled away.

And at midnight Nico woke up hard and pressed against her, so he turned onto his back and tried to think boring, unsexy thoughts.

It was a joke that they'd pretended either of them would sleep. Nico wanted sex. And the woman he wanted to have sex with lay beside him. He could feel her desire in the thick air between them.

Yet sex could only muddy the waters.

He could tell that she was awake next to him.

'Nico?' she said. 'We have to talk…'

She said it as if *he* was the one who was reluctant— as if *he* was the one who had shut down the conversation two hours ago.

Life with Aurora!

But he didn't bother pointing it out, for indeed it *was* time to talk, to work things out. Here in the dark.

'What do you want to happen, Aurora?'

'I don't know.'

'You must have thought about it or at least considered it.'

'I'm confused,' she admitted, and when he took her hand, she squeezed his back.

'Then let's talk it out.'

'From what I can see I have two options.'

'Options are good—so tell me.'

'I want to tell you…' She just did not know how.

But as she lay in the darkness she found a way, and she spoke to him as she had to Louanna the night before Gabe had been born.

'I wanted to tell—' She had been about to say, *to tell you*, but held it in. 'From the moment I found out I was pregnant I wanted to tell the baby's father. After all, there is no doubt that Gabe is his. And I believe he would support the baby.'

'Of course he would,' Nico answered carefully. He would give the world to get her real thoughts, and if taking himself out of the equation helped, then that was fine with him.

'But I worry,' Aurora said, 'that he might suggest the other option.'

Nico was silent.

'Marriage,' she said. 'You see, he turned me down once, and I would always feel I had forced him into it.'

'Okay…'

It was a gentle *okay*. It gave no indication as to his thoughts. More an acknowledgment that he had heard her.

'I think,' Aurora said, 'that he will want the second option—even if he doesn't *really* want it. He's a good man, and very respected by my family. They would certainly expect him to marry me.'

'And you don't want that?'

'No. I think I would prefer option one.'

'Okay…?'

It was the same response as before, but it contained a question.

'You see,' Aurora ventured, 'I think he might regret that day.'

'Well, I don't think he does.'

'I mean, he never wanted to marry…'

Silence from Nico.

'But now he will try to do the right thing by me. I would hate that. I think our marriage would be a terrible mistake.' She struggled to voice the picture that danced in her mind. 'He would come to Silibri and see us now and then…perhaps at weekends…and then return to his life. I would have a husband and Gabe a father and we would have respect in the village, and he would have his life in Roma. His stunning apartment and…' She did not finish.

'And?' Nico pushed.

'Other women.'

Her breath was held tight in her lungs as he seemed to consider it.

'You'd be okay with that?' Nico checked.

And because it was dark she could not see his smile. And because she was so focussed on the awful scenario that danced in her mind she did not hear the tiny tease in his words.

She missed, completely, the fact that Nico had made a joke.

'Of course not,' she snapped.

'Do you love him, Aurora?'

'Too much.'

'Do you believe he loves you?'

'If he does it is a very occasional love—not enough to endure a lifetime. Which is why I prefer option one.'

'You will *always* have option one, where he supports both you and the baby, but what of option two?' Nico persisted. 'What if he wants marriage and a family now? What if he has changed his mind?'

'Perhaps he is just saying that to humour me. You see, I know for a fact he would prefer a quiet wife who would stay in the background...'

'You know that for a *fact*?'

'Yes!' Aurora said. 'Because he told me so himself. And I'm not so good at being the type of wife he prefers. I could try to be her, though...'

'Why would you try to be someone you're not?'

'Because if he makes the effort for me, then I should do the same for him.'

'Would he want you to change?'

'He wants serene, he wants elegant, and he wants

calm and peace.' She turned and looked at him in the darkness. 'I could try to be all of that.'

'You won't last five minutes, Aurora.'

'Watch me, Nico.'

He did.

Nico watched her sleep.

CHAPTER FOURTEEN

GABE!

Aurora woke in an empty bed and no baby.

No Nico.

Yes, she had the nanny, but panic had her dashing down the grand stairs and through the long entrance hall—and then coming to a halt at the door of the kitchen.

Nico sat on a bar stool holding her baby—or rather, *their* baby. He was wearing suit trousers, socks and shoes, but he was naked from the hips up and unshaven.

Half executive, half temptation.

'I overslept,' Aurora said. 'I never oversleep.'

'It's only seven.'

'That's late for me. Usually I'm up at six…sometimes five…' She was gabbling. But she had to keep speaking about inane things because the sight of him, the delicious sight of him, was too much for this hour.

'Gabe needs to be fed,' Aurora said, holding out her hands for him to hand over their son.

'I just fed him,' Nico said. 'And that is why I am not wearing a shirt. He vomited on me. The nanny is sorting me out another one.'

'Oh.' Aurora didn't know what to say to that, but

again held her hands out for her son. 'Well, he needs to be changed.'

'He's already been changed,' Nico said.

'Did you do that too?'

'No.' Nico shook his head. 'I left that to the nanny.'

He smiled, and it was so rare that he did, that when he did she felt as if she wore skates and the marble floor was ice, for she wanted to glide over to Nico.

Her outstretched hands were now for *him*, Aurora realised, so she dropped them to her sides.

'He's handsome,' Nico said, looking down at his son.

'Very.'

'I would expect his father must be too,' Nico said, slipping into the banter they had shared last night.

'Not really.' Aurora wrinkled her nose and teased him, but could not erase her smile. She tried to, but it just kept shining through.

And then it dawned on her how terrible she must look, in his crumpled shirt and with a bruise on her cheek. Surely his perfect wife would be in active wear at this hour, all glowing from her morning yoga—or from having just gone down on him.

Aurora preferred the thought of the latter, even if she had never done it before…

'I'd better go,' Nico said.

'Where?' Aurora asked.

'Where do you think?'

'Can't work wait, Nico? Surely we have a lot to discuss and—' She halted herself, for she had sworn at least to try and be the perfect wife. 'What time will you be…?' She swallowed. His perfect wife would not ask when he would be back. 'I'm going to cook today.'

'I have a housekeeper for that.'

Although then he realised that she and her husband had both just gone on leave.

'Or I have chefs down the road,' Nico said. 'And, anyway, you need to shop.'

'Why?'

'Because you need new clothes. And a haircut.' He picked up her hand. 'And a manicure, my dear elegant wife.'

She had never in her life had a manicure.

'I don't have time for that. I have a son to take care of.'

'And a husband to please…?' Then he stopped teasing her. 'You have taken care of our son alone for the last two months, so today is for you. Go to the boutiques at the hotel and then to the salon. I shall let them know to expect you.'

'Nico, I can't—'

'You never have to say that again, Aurora.'

But he was not saying it with the tender care she needed this morning. He was not holding her in his arms and telling her the nightmare of her world without him was over.

Instead, he was basically telling her that the money was taken care of.

Which was nice, of course. But it wasn't even the icing on the cake. It was like a sugar ball that rotted your teeth and stuck in your throat.

She could not bear to spend the day without him— without knowing what went on in his head and what his reaction was to the fears she had shared last night.

'I could come and see you on your lunchbreak?' she suggested.

'Aurora, I don't *have* a lunchbreak.'

'Is that only for peasants?' she sneered.

'Yep.'

'Well, I might bring Gabe up to your office…'

'No.' He shook his head. 'You need a day off to take care of yourself. Anyway, I'm too busy today.' He glanced at the time. 'I really had better go…'

Finally he handed her Gabe, and looked right into her eyes. For a second she thought he might kiss her, but it was a fleeting second, for he'd already pulled back.

'You need to shave,' Aurora said.

'Funny, that, because suddenly I don't have time.'

The nanny came in then, with another shirt. He dressed hastily and left.

Oh, what had she done…?

She looked at the baby bottle on the kitchen bench, at the dinner plates and wine glasses still on the dinner table from last night, and she thought of her dishevelled appearance and all the chaos she had brought into his supremely ordered life.

Nico was a man who liked order and calm.

Well, he would get it, Aurora decided. He would come home tonight to the fabled perfect wife.

Nico would get the woman he truly wanted.

'Aurora!'

Luigi greeted her like a long-lost friend. 'Marianna called and said you were coming in! It is so wonderful to see you again.'

'I look terrible,' Aurora grumbled as she sat in a chair in the luxurious salon. She looked so sallow in the mirror that she barely recognised herself.

'What happened to your cheek? You poor thing!'

'I got in the way of an angry man and his wife,' Aurora admitted.

'Well, Luigi is going to wave his magic wand and make you all better.'

'Can you make me elegant, Luigi?'

'Of course. I can do anything.'

Make him love me, Aurora thought as she handed herself over to Luigi and his minions.

It was *not* a little job.

She received a facial and, of all things, eyelash extensions. And a manicure. And a pedicure. All this before he even got to work on her make-up and hair.

And they chatted.

'What should I wear?'

'In the boutique next door,' Luigi told her, 'there is a grey chiffon dress... Oh, my, Aurora, it is so elegant.'

'Grey?'

'I shall call them now and have them bring it round for you to view it.'

It was very lovely—but very grey.

'Do you have it in red?'

'Aurora...' Luigi warned her.

Oh, that was right—she was to stand in the corner, fade into the background and pour his martini.

She would wear the grey.

And pearl drops for earrings, but please not these rather demure mid-height heels.

'They are very...' Aurora sat in the beauty chair as the boutique owner touted his wares and she slipped the shoes on her feet. 'Plain.'

'They are perfect, Aurora,' Luigi assured her as he finally got to work on her hair.

And Gabe was not left out.

He was a rich baby now, and he had a pretty powder-blue suit to look the part. And little powder-blue booties and a white silk bib.

She was getting good at this, Aurora thought as she arrived home at four, with her new eyelashes and nails, and lashings of make-up, and her hair in a gorgeous chignon.

'Oh, *bella*!' the nanny said. 'Look at you!'

'Thank you.' Aurora took the compliment with a smile. 'I'm going to get my new dress on soon and…' She looked around. 'Where is the housekeeper?'

'I don't know.'

'But what about dinner?' Aurora asked, and went down the hall and looked at the gleaming table, still littered with last night's plates. 'And the table needs to be dressed. I didn't even make the bed.'

She looked urgently to the nanny, who gave her the nicest smile.

'I don't do housework,' she said.

'Of course not.' Aurora said. 'But—'

'In any way shape or form.'

'Good…good…' Aurora said.

It was no problem.

And, despite having to get through a lot of domestic duties, she would *not* be ringing the hotel for their dinner. That would be ridiculous when Aurora loved to cook.

And so she made the bed, and tidied the room, and life felt much as it had when she had been a cleaner in Silibri.

Except now she wore a gorgeous dress and had pretty eyes and nails. She cleared the plates and set the table, and went down to his cellar and chose some wine—which was easy for a girl who had grown up surrounded by vines.

But time was creeping on.

She put on an apron and found luck was on her

side—because the *passata* she had bought Nico a year ago was still in the cupboard. And *passata* only got better with age!

One day she might take a course, so she would better be able to create the fancy dishes that Nico must like, but for now she would cook the way she knew how.

But there was no meat in his massive bare fridge. And by the time she got back from the butcher it was getting really late.

However, the pasta was made and had been cut into ribbons, and the sauce was bubbling away as she bathed Gabe and then dressed him.

'Look at you…' Aurora smiled at her chubby baby. His black hair was damp from the bath and he wore a pale blue sleepsuit and a gummy smile. 'Daddy will be back soon…'

Her voice trailed off. For Nico had left this morning, just after seven, and it was now dark—and he had not so much as texted, let alone called.

With her perfect baby lying on the bed, Aurora took off her apron and changed into the plain grey shoes and smoothed the elegant grey dress. She topped up her lipstick and then carried Gabe downstairs, taking dainty steps just in case Nico arrived.

The scent of *passata* filled the house, the aroma of herbs and the garlic making her stomach growl. Everything was in perfect order. The pasta just needed a couple of moments in boiling water and dinner would be ready.

When he came home.

'Perhaps I should text and see where he is,' Aurora said to little Gabe, but he stared back at her with huge navy eyes that were turning black, like his father's, and she remembered that Nico's perfect wife would not do such a thing.

She would *accept* that he was working when he was late.

Gabe started to rub his eyes and grizzle.

'He's tired,' the nanny said.

'He's okay,' Aurora insisted.

She wanted Nico to come home to a stunning Aurora and a gleaming, smiling baby.

'Why don't I put him down to sleep?' the nanny asked a full hour later. Gabe clearly wanted to lay down his head and he had been sick on his lovely pale blue suit. 'You can have your nice meal and relax…'

'No!' Aurora said, for she wanted to sleep beside her baby.

But then she remembered the new rules that she was enforcing. A calm house, a serene and smiling Aurora…

How it ached to hand Gabe over—and then, for the first time in eight weeks, she was alone.

Eight weeks and nine months—for she had loved Gabe even when he'd lived inside her.

And Aurora loved fiercely.

She could feel snakes of anger rising in her chest as she sat there in the lounge, tapping her grey-shod foot as the night wore on. Finally she caved, and called him—but of course his phone was off.

So she called the hotel, and was eventually put through to a weary-sounding Marianna.

'Signor Caruso is not here, Aurora.'

'What time did he leave work?'

'He hasn't been in today.'

Her new shoes hurt, so she took them off. Her new eyelashes itched as she took the *passata* off the stove and then decided she was starving and cooked the pasta.

He could reheat his own.

The louse.

She had told him of her love, and she had shared her dark fears. And his response?

Silence.

Always, always silence from Nico, when she needed his thoughts the most.

Argh!

She threw the spaghetti at the wall—and not to check if it might stick! She threw it in frustration, in despair and in pain—because she wanted this to stop.

For this love for Nico to fade.

For the depth of her soul, where he resided, to be excised, so that she could move on with her life with her head held high.

It was nearly midnight as she sat at the dinner table and wept—because *this* was her life. Loving a man who did not so much as call.

Perhaps he was out with his lover. Breaking it off with her because, sorry, he'd just found out he was a father...

Maybe they were making love now.

Break-up sex.

Which would lead to make-up sex when he weakened and grew bored with his Silibrian mountain girl.

'I hate you, Nico Caruso!' she wept.

'Of course you do.'

And there he was, standing in the doorway, looking a whole lot more crumpled than he had that morning but still with plenty of dash.

'Where *were* you?' Aurora demanded as she stood up. 'Marianna said you have not been in work today.'

'When you calm down I will tell you.'

'Don't tell me to calm down. You have a son now—

you have responsibilities—' She could have bitten off her tongue, and yet she could not stop, and now huge angry tears were spilling out. 'You stay out to this time of night like an alley cat! It is not a good example to set for your son.' She let out the hurt that was really on her mind. 'I told you I loved you, Nico. I gave you all my fears and you gave me nothing back. I will never forgive you for that!'

'Never?' he checked.

'Never, *ever*!'

She could feel her hair, uncoiled and spilling over her face, and she knew her make-up was smeared just when she wanted to be so calm and serene.

'Never!'

She jabbed a finger at his chest, but he caught it and pulled her into him, and kissed her hard, his mouth smothering hers.

She pulled her face back. 'Don't you dare kiss me to keep me quiet,' she said, but she made only a half-hearted effort to push him off. 'Anyway, you still haven't shaved. You will cut my face to ribbons...'

'You wanted a man with a beard, Aurora.'

'Perhaps—but I want a man who is devoted. I want a man who does not tell me he's in the office—'

His reply was to haul her over his shoulder.

'You wanted a man to come home to a house in chaos and laugh and then spank you.'

'Nico, no!' She was wriggling, and she did not know what was happening, but then he let her down, slowly against his chest.

He did not let her go; he held her tightly in his arms. 'Good, because I could never spank a woman—let alone the woman I love.'

She missed the moment. It was just so impossible that her mind brushed it off.

'Oh, the woman you love? Did you say that to your redhead? Did you say that to your blonde?'

Nico had the audacity to laugh.

'It's not funny, Nico—how *could* you?'

'As it turned out, I couldn't.' He was the accusing one now. 'You've not only messed with my head but with my prowess, Aurora.'

'Liar.'

'It's true,' Nico said. 'There's been no one since you.' And then he amended that a touch. 'The *second* time around.'

That should have made her rage, but then she saw the intense look in his eyes, and she realised that in the midst of all this he had told her he loved her—that in these past agonising months there had been no one but her.

'Don't tell me you love me unless you mean it,' she begged.

'I do mean it.'

He was breathing hard and he put his hands gently on her cheeks. His thumbs wiped away her tears and he made her look at him.

'I love you, Aurora, and you were wrong last night. This is not an occasional love—it's an endless love. Over and over I told myself that I didn't want it, but it turns out that I do.'

'Why would you not want love?' Aurora asked.

She thought she had already worked out the answer, but she needed to hear it from Nico.

'I never knew how good it could be,' Nico said. 'I thought life would be better lived for the most part alone.'

For look what love had done to him.

'I thought it was better to stay back,' he explained. 'But of course I couldn't. I always wondered if it was guilt or duty that pulled me back to Silibri—I could not decide between the two. But it was neither. It was love—my love for *you*.'

And then came that almost grim smile. The one she was getting to know. The one that meant Nico might lose his head at any given time.

It was a gesture she could read and it was a little more that she knew about this remote man.

A shiver that ran through her as she thought how much more there was to know, and that soon he would ravish her.

He lifted her onto the granite bench, so she was at eye level with him. She looked deep into his black eyes...

One day she would count those thick dark lashes, Aurora decided. One day, when she could hold off for a moment, she would count every last one.

But there was no holding back for Nico.

There should be sparks between them, Aurora thought as his mouth moved to claim hers. He was kissing her so hard it was as if he had been starving for her—as if the air in her mouth was the air he needed to breathe.

It wasn't elegant sex.

Nor was it serene.

She kissed him back—not just his mouth but his face, his eyes, his neck. She gave up trying to undo his shirt and moved down to his belt, but Nico had already taken care of that.

She looked down and saw him, huge and aroused. His impatient hands were tearing at her sophisticated underwear as he berated her for wearing knickers when he had to have her *now*.

'Is it too soon after…?'

He was trying to slow down even as he tore the last items off…even as he confirmed that she was ready with his fingers. He was trying to be measured and controlled and…well, a responsible new father.

'It's not soon enough,' she moaned. 'Are *we* sorted, though?'

She meant the Nico loving her thing—for it was all too new and too much to fully take in.

'We're sorted,' he told her.

And then he slipped slowly inside her, stretching her and filling her as only Nico could.

And then his hands were everywhere, shredding the flimsy dress, baring her breasts as he had wanted to on that first day in Rome.

He was the man she had first made love to—he was Nico unleashed and untamed—and he was everything Aurora needed tonight.

She *wanted* the fierce possession of his kiss, and she *wanted* the full power of Nico Caruso.

And he gave it.

Over and over and over.

She felt as hot in his hands as she had when the mountains had been ablaze in Sicily that night. And she felt as safe as she had been on that cold morning in Rome when she'd looked up into his eyes.

'I've kept on wanting you,' she told him as he thrust into her and dug his fingers into her hips.

He turned the blood in her veins into champagne and he took her body to places that would have otherwise remained unseen and unknown.

'Aurora!' he said, and his voice sounded like a car skidding and careering on gravel.

Aurora felt just as out of control until she heard the delicious sound of Nico calling her name.

'Nico...'

She wrapped her legs tight around him and buried her face in his neck, inhaling the scent of Nico aroused. It was the scent she craved from the man she adored and she wanted to linger there a moment, to imprint that scent combined with the delicious feel of Nico unleashed upon her, but then she felt a lurch inside her and the swell of him within.

He *summoned* an orgasm from her. He simply demanded it—this very instant.

The tears and frustrations of the day seemed to gather and tighten, pulling her into a frenzied peak, and Aurora sobbed in frustration—for she simply did not know what to do with all the love she had for this man.

Except give it to him.

So much for elegance.

Nico helped Aurora down from the bench and then zipped himself up. He pocketed her bra and knickers to save the nanny finding them.

And then he surveyed the chaos.

There was spaghetti on the wall, and he felt the *thump, thump* of his swelling heart as he looked in the pot on the stove and smelt the herbs and the garlic, and saw the remains of the perfect dinner she had prepared for them.

No, not exactly elegant. But he warmed it up, and she grated pecorino cheese, and then they ate standing up. Like two filthy beggars, they shared what was left in the pot.

'Your father was right,' Nico said.

'I'm not talking to my father,' Aurora said.

'But he was right about one thing,' Nico said, as he wiped a little bit of *passata* from her chin. '"Good food and family and my day is complete. What more could I want?"'

'You should raise your voice a little when impersonating my father,' Aurora said.

'But I wasn't impersonating him.'

CHAPTER FIFTEEN

HE TOOK HER TO BED.

And he did not close the drapes.

They just lay there, sated and spent, with her head on his chest, his fingers playing idly with her hair, and the steady *thump, thump* of their hearts.

Aurora still had many questions, and she could not stop herself asking the important one. 'Nico, where have you been all day?' She looked up at him with urgent eyes. 'And until so late in the night.'

She simply *had* to know.

'Where do you think I've been, Aurora?'

'You don't want to know my thoughts. In them you have been to many places.'

'Okay—where do you think a man goes when the love of his life shows up?'

She went pale in his arms.

'I went to Silibri to speak with your father.'

'You have told him that Gabe is yours?'

'Of course I have.'

Nico was quiet for a moment, for it had taken great restraint not to tear into Bruno and his wife for their treatment of Aurora. He could not stand to think of all they had put their daughter through when she had needed them the most.

But they would soon be family, and he had chosen to remember that.

'What did he say?'

'He huffed and puffed,' Nico said.

'And Mamma?'

He could hear the anguish in Aurora's voice.

'She asked how you were and then she started crying. She asked me what Gabe looked like.'

'Yet all she had to do to find out was pick up the phone.'

'Of course,' Nico said. 'But they spoke of your dating app...'

Aurora did not laugh.

'It was confusing for them,' he said gently. 'And then your father got out a bottle of—'

'Limoncello.' Aurora finished his sentence for him.

'I always wondered why he did not stop speaking to me after I refused to marry you,' Nico admitted.

'And me,' Aurora agreed. 'I thought your name would be mud in our house, but he kept insisting you join us.'

'He said he would believe that I had not offended you unless I married someone else. But if I did then all bets would be off.' He smiled as Aurora laughed. 'He knew,' Nico said. 'He knew, that night when you headed out to the party, that I was churning inside.'

'I would hope he does not know what occurred on the sofa.'

'Of course not—or I would be dead. And anyway, a nice girl like you would never...' He looked over and smiled.

'Aurora, he brought out the Grappa he had been saving for this moment.'

'You told him you were marrying me?'

'No,' Nico said. 'I told him that I wanted, more than anything, to marry his daughter. And then I told him we had stuff to sort out first.'

'Nico, don't make a mistake,' Aurora said. 'I am strong.'

'I know you are.'

'And if you marry me then you will get the full force of my love.'

'Aurora,' he said, very definitely, 'you will get the full force of mine.'

'All I want, Nico, is the full force of your love.'

It was all she had ever wanted, and she felt as if it had been fully received—but those worms of doubt had started wriggling, and then, from the other side of this vast house, she heard a tiny wail.

Was it Gabe he was here for?

'I have to go to him,' Aurora said.

'I know,' Nico agreed.

Even though there was the nanny he had had checked and re-checked a hundred times over. She was the very best nanny, and she would love both mother and infant, but she did not do housework.

In any way shape or form.

'Gabe…' Aurora walked into the comfy lounge, where her son was being winded midway through his bottle. 'I'll give him the second half,' she said. 'And then put him down again.'

He seemed to have grown in the time he'd been here, Aurora thought as she fed him, and she looked into eyes that could not be called navy any more.

They were black.

'Your father,' Aurora said, 'is the most complicated man I know.'

She looked at her son for a very long time.

At the long fingers that clutched hers as she fed him.

At his lashes, which she had already counted.

Then at the perfect dent in his jaw.

'I love him and I believe he loves me...' she whispered, and her breath hitched. 'Not a hundred percent as yet, and not as fiercely as I love him, but, my dear son, I do believe he is trying to love our little family.'

She knew eight years of rejection could not be eradicated in one night.

Aurora padded back to the bedroom and Nico could see that she had cried. It twisted him up inside that his cold, unwilling heart had hurt her.

'We'll build a house in Silibri,' Nico said as she climbed back into bed.

'And you will fly back to Rome...'

'No,' Nico said, '*we* will fly back to Rome. We will be based in Silibri, though.'

'No.'

Her emphatic *no* surprised them both. It was immediate, even though she had never dared to give a future with Nico true thought.

Aurora loved Silibri very much, but though there were so many decent memories she could think of, there were old hurts that resided there for Nico, and current ones for Aurora too, for her parents had turned their backs when she had needed them the most.

'We'll be based here, Nico,' she said. 'I want to sleep most nights in the bed where Gabe was made, and I want to wake to the Villa Borghese Park outside my window.'

'You're sure?'

'Very,' Aurora said, and then thought about it some more. 'We'll go back often,' she added, and then she looked over to him. 'And, of course, I would like to manage the temple weddings.'

'You don't give in, do you?'

'Never,' Aurora said. 'Not when I know I am right.'

She had tried to give up on their love so many times and to let Nico go. She thought of her tears, and the coin-toss at the Trevi Fountain when she had begged to be made love to in Rome.

'I want that job, Nico.'

'Then you shall have it.'

'I don't want favours, though,' she said as she lay in his bed. 'I really am the best for that role.'

She was also, Aurora knew, the best for his heart.

CHAPTER SIXTEEN

'LISTEN TO ME, NICO…'

Of all the bizarre moments in Nico's life, this possibly earned top billing: Pino giving him marital advice.

As it turned out, Nico *wasn't* the last in his family.

He still had many of them. Not blood relatives, perhaps, but neither would he introduce them as friends, for they were so much more.

'You have to keep the romance,' Pino said. 'I have been married to Rosa for thirty years, so listen when I give you advice. Even if it has not been a good day, you have to find a way to enjoy the night.'

'I can do that.' Nico nodded.

'And you have to dance,' Francesca added. 'Often.'

But Nico dismissed that suggestion with a shake of his head. 'I don't dance.'

It was three hours until sunset, and while Aurora was having all her treatments in the oratory, he was in the café on the hill with the Silibri contingent.

'Aurora can dance. She can dance very well,' Francesca said. 'You cannot let her down.'

And who knew that Vincenzo just happened to have been a ballroom champion, or a tango master, or something along those lines, a decade ago?

But Vincenzo wasn't a kind teacher.

Vincenzo was impatient, and exacting, and Nico could never have imagined he would spend the hours before his wedding dancing with a man in a butterscotch suit.

'And there will be the tarantella,' Francesca said.

Nico frowned. He'd rather avoided weddings.

Until now.

Luigi had been brought in for this very special day, but instead of an elegant chignon, or snaky curls, Aurora chose to wear her hair loose and long.

Her make-up was for the most part subtle, but she asked Luigi to go to town with the eyeliner.

'Not just yet,' Luigi said, and glanced up. 'There's a surprise for you!'

'What?'

And then through the doors came Antonietta.

'Oh!'

'Don't cry,' Antonietta warned as they embraced.

She wanted to, though, for it had been four long years with just the occasional message in between. 'I never thought you'd come today!' Aurora said.

'I nearly didn't,' Antonietta admitted. 'But I could not stay away from your wedding.'

'Have you seen any of your family since you've been back?'

'Don't worry about that now,' Antonietta said. 'You have a wedding to attend. I'm going to head down to the ruins, but I just wanted to give you a kiss and offer my best wishes. Now, in case I don't stay for the party after, here...' She handed Aurora a little silver medal. 'For you to carry with you today.'

It was a French good luck charm: *Bonheur*, the little medal said.

'It means happiness,' Antonietta explained. 'That is my wish for you.'

Aurora thought back to that night on the hillside, watching the fires coming for them, and the wise counsel her friend had given her when she had told her to go home.

Aurora was so glad she had.

'I will carry it with me for ever. And I wish the same for you,' Aurora said.

But she felt the fragile shoulders beneath her hand and looked into her friend's sad eyes. It was an almost futile wish, Aurora was sure.

No!

She would never give up on her friend.

'We are going to catch up properly soon,' Aurora said as tears sparkled in her eyes. 'Even if I have to come to France to do so.'

'You *will* have to come to France,' Antonietta said, 'for I am no longer welcome here.' And then she recovered. 'Get on with your wedding! Your Nico is waiting...'

'My heart is waiting,' Aurora corrected. 'And I will tell this only to you. I think he almost loves me. And I believe that Nico will be the best father in the world.'

She blew at an escaped curl that Luigi would have to attend to in a moment. But right now she spoke honestly to her friend.

'He tells me that I am mad to doubt him...'

'Aurora...' Antonietta said.

She braced herself for a pep talk from her friend, for Antonietta to tell her that of *course* she was not mad. That of *course* she should enter this marriage with a reasonable nugget of doubt as to Nico's love.

But Antonietta had long ago thrown away the script.

'You *are* mad,' Antonietta said. 'Nico loves you. Why can't you just accept it?'

It was a good question.

It had been wonderful to see her friend, although Aurora was very pleased that Luigi hadn't applied the eyeliner before Antonietta had arrived.

'You are ready,' Luigi said to the bride.

He had indeed waved his magic wand—but not too much, for it was happiness that shone through on this day.

'Oh, Aurora…' Her father beamed when he saw her. 'This is the best day of my life,' he said. 'I always knew he was right for you…'

It would be easy for her to hold a grudge. But her parents doted on Gabe and had been all over Aurora from the second they'd found out that the baby was Nico's. They seemed to have conveniently forgotten that they had forced their pregnant daughter to leave home.

Forgiveness was not always the easier path. It was spiky and it stung as you trod on old hurts and raged internally.

'It's not worth it, Aurora,' Nico had said as he'd held her hands and she had sobbed in frustration.

And she had looked up to a master. She had looked up to and learned from a man who had been beaten, but who had risen.

Yes, forgiveness was a spiky path, but if you pushed on and through it you got to those bulrushes, waiting to be snapped so that a million seeds of kindness could escape…

And so, instead of pointing out the hurts her father had caused, when Bruno said he had always known Nico was the one for his daughter, Aurora smiled and agreed. 'You did always say that, Pa.'

It was better to be kind today.

And it was easy to be happy.

Especially when Nadia and Antonio ran in, laughing, carrying a small posy of the freshly picked wild flowers that Aurora would carry.

'You look pretty,' Nadia said.

'So do you,' Aurora said. She smiled and looked at Antonio. 'And you look so handsome! Your *mamma* is going to be so proud when she sees you at the temple ruins.'

Nico had arranged for them to come to the wedding, and they were both Aurora's flower-pickers and her little escorts on the walk to the temple.

And as she walked towards the ruins on her father's arm the resentment slid away, for there was nowhere more calming nor more beautiful than the temple ruins at sunset...

Aurora had been absolutely right about the staff uniforms, because Persian Orange was the colour of this night.

As well as cinnamon, and gold, plus a thousand unnamed shades of orange with which the sky blazed.

And orange did not give Nico a headache tonight.

Pino nudged him needlessly, to say that his bride was here.

Her dress was white, and fell in heavy drapes, and to Nico she looked like a goddess walking towards him.

Aurora cared not for the eyebrow-raises of certain people in the village, who were clucking behind their hands at the audacity of a single mother wearing white.

It was *her* wedding.

The day of which she had dreamt.

Only it was better than her dreams. For in those they

had not been at the temple, and Nico had not smiled at his bride the way he did on this day approaching night.

In her earlier dreams Nico had been a whole lot younger and perhaps, she conceded, just a touch less certain. On this new night and for evermore she was his chosen one. Of that she was ninety-nine-point-nine percent certain.

The whisper of doubt was so tiny in comparison that sense and hope combined to make her believe that Nico wanted this just as much as she did.

'Aurora and Nico,' said the celebrant, 'we stand today amidst these ancient ruins to celebrate your unending love.'

And it *was* both unending and without a clear beginning, for neither could quite pin down when their love had commenced.

When she'd used to open the door and tease him with 'Hello, husband'?

Or when Nico had denied to himself the fact that tears had pooled in her eyes when he had told her he would never marry?

Had there been love there that night on her father's sofa?

And had it returned again on the night Gabe had been made?

Or had it never left them?

It was Nico who answered as he pushed the ring on her finger. 'I have always loved you.'

First he had loved her like a sister, and for a while they had failed as friends. But they were friends now. And they were lovers and partners and parents too.

'And I always shall,' Nico said, looking right into those dark velvet eyes. There was nothing more beautiful than this beautiful Sicilian woman.

And now it was Aurora's turn to speak, and to push her ring onto his finger. 'I tried so hard not to love you,' she told him, and the world. 'I can stop fighting with myself now. I love you, Nico Caruso.'

'And I love *you*, Aurora Eloise Caruso.'

'Finally!' She smiled as her groom kissed his bride.

Nico was not a sociable person, and Aurora was not expecting a wild party. But back at the hotel the champagne flowed, and he accepted the many congratulations and danced with his bride.

Nico *danced*!

He pulled her in, he twirled her—and he even, to Aurora's delight, dipped her.

She laughed. 'Where did you learn that?' she asked. And even before the burn of jealousy could take her over, that he might have learned it in the arms of another woman, Nico halted her.

'Vincenzo taught me.'

'No!'

'*Sì!*'

The Silibri contingent saw the smiles and the near-kiss and started clinking their spoons on their glasses, demanding that Nico and Aurora proceed.

Oh, his kiss was heaven.

Just heavenly.

Deep and slow and loving.

And Aurora was starting to let go of that tiny little percentage of worry that Nico might not be as on board with this as she.

She could never be an actress, she knew, for she let her emotions carry her away. While Nico, on the other hand…

But this kiss was both silk and velvet, and it was at her own wedding party, which she had dreamed of.

It was Aurora who wanted to leave and go to bed...

But then it started.

A huge circle was forming, and she and Nico were being pushed into the middle.

'The tarantella,' Aurora informed him, still sure that weddings were not his thing.

'I know what it is, Aurora.'

He spun her as the circle moved in and out, with laughter and dancing, friends and family. The music pushed them to dance faster, and Nico never missed a beat.

Nico pulled her into him, and even in the midst of a circle full of joy and laughter he read in the woman he loved a sense of duty.

No glass would go unfilled tonight.

And no smile would be unreturned.

In a few moments he would take her upstairs and make love to her, as expected, but there was no sense of duty there.

How did he tell this complex woman that neither guilt nor duty could have him dancing the tarantella with such glee tonight?

Nico even held her hands as they were jumping. Stood in the middle of a circle doing silly jumping claps as the accordion insisted they jump some more.

This was a husband she had never seen before.

And Aurora really had to get him to a bed!

'My wife is tired,' Nico explained as they left. 'Party on.'

Aurora kissed her tiny son, who had been an absolute angel and would be treated like a prince in her parents' home tonight.

'I love you,' she said to Gabe. 'And I love your father so, so much.'

'Come on,' Nico said, and he took her hand.

There would be celebrations aplenty tonight, if he knew this lot, but right now he wanted his wife alone.

He led her up the winding stairs and she went to walk through the cloister, but he pulled her back. 'This way.'

'Aren't we staying in the Temple Suite?' Aurora checked, for it was the suite they both loved and the view that felt like theirs.

'Not tonight,' Nico said. 'In case you've forgotten, this is our honeymoon.'

Oh!

For all she had pored over the pictures and been on board with the renovations, she had a blind spot when it came to the Honeymoon Suite. So certain that she would never stay there.

Or, worse, that she might be there with a reluctant groom.

But now she stepped in and it was Aurora who gasped—for she had seen it by day, but never at night.

It was one Silibri's best-kept secrets.

'Oh, Nico!'

The glass domed ceiling revealed the stars and the Sicilian night sky.

'And do you know,' Nico said, 'that there are steps down to a private beach?'

'I wrote the brochure, Nico,' she teased.

But in truth she was in awe. How did a boy from Silibri, even if he'd inherited the land, do all this?

For there was magic in this building.

'It should be called the Starlight Suite,' Aurora said. 'And you know I'm right.'

'Of course you are,' Nico said, 'and that is why I have a present for you.'

Aurora frowned as he went over to a tray, where an ice bucket was cooling a bottle of champagne, but it was not that which he brought over. Instead it was a small pouch that he handed to her.

'Keys?' Aurora frowned as they fell into her palm. 'Is this to your home in Rome? Because I thought that was all electronic—'

'Aurora, look at them.'

They were old keys. One was thick and heavy, the type you might use to open a gate.

The gate at the side of her *nonna*'s house…

'Nico?' She did not understand. 'You've bought Nonna's house?'

'I bought your *nonna*'s house many months ago—through a third party, so your father wouldn't know it was me. Aurora, the only draw about my staying in Silibri was the thought that at night I would come home to you…'

Aurora looked at the heavy keys she held in her palm and laughed. 'Nico, the only thing that kept me sane in Silibri was the fact that one day I would marry you.'

'I love you,' he told her again. Aurora had always been his fabled wife.

'You really bought the cottage?'

She held the keys now. Or rather, they shared them.

'I bought the cottage, Aurora. At the time I didn't know why, but I do now—I guess I didn't want that dream of being with you to die completely.'

'But…' She looked at him. 'You said you could think of nothing worse than living opposite my parents.'

'And I still can't,' Nico admitted. 'But for holidays, and for things like Christmas, when there are too many

Messinas in your parents' house, we can just head over the road to our own little home. And for the times when we are fed up with the hotel...'

And Aurora's tiny, grating percentage of doubt faded under a million Sicilian stars and the softest kiss.

'Tomorrow,' Nico said as he removed her dress and her pretty underwear, 'we will take the steps down to the beach and I am going to have you in the water.'

'What about now?' She liked the thought of a naked swim, but Nico was already laying her down.

'No, no,' he said, and parted her legs, ready to dive into her. 'For tonight, all you have to do is look to the stars.'

* * * * *